THE
WHITE
HORSE
INN

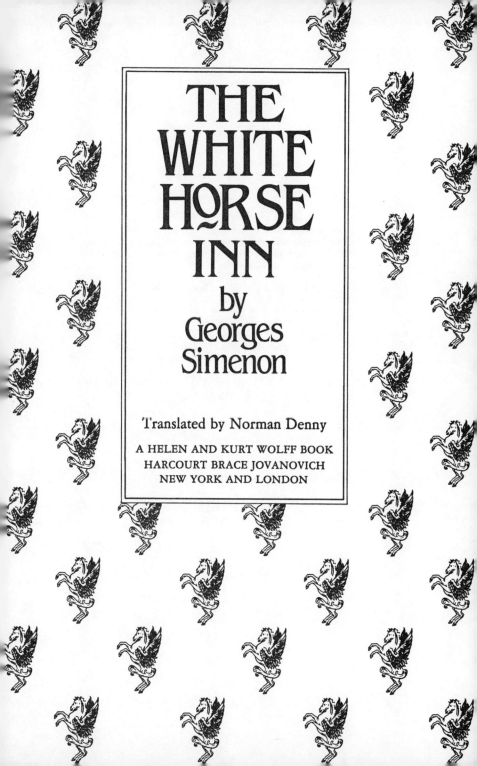

THE WHITE HORSE INN

by
Georges Simenon

Translated by Norman Denny

A HELEN AND KURT WOLFF BOOK
HARCOURT BRACE JOVANOVICH
NEW YORK AND LONDON

Printed in the United States of America

Library of Congress Cataloging in Publication Data

Simenon, Georges, 1903–
The White Horse Inn.
Translation of Le Cheval Blanc.
"A Helen and Kurt Wolff book."
I. Title.
PZ3.S5892Wg   1980   [PQ2637.I53]   843'.912   79-3363
ISBN 0-15-196240-5

First edition
B C D E

1

"You should put him down, Maurice."

Why that phrase rather than any other? And why that particular minute rather than any other minute on that Pentecostal Sunday?

The little boy made no attempt to understand. He did not know that this was to be important to him, that the picture of his father then registered in his mind would be the only one that he would recall later, when he was grown up, and perhaps later still, when he was an old man.

He looked up, because he was only seven years old, and his father seemed to him extraordinarily tall, his height increased by Christian, who was seated astride his shoulders, and by the shadow cast by the setting sun.

"At least give me your hat, or he'll ruin it."

For Christian was clutching his father's hat with both hands. He was not excited and did not consider that to be carried this way was a game.

Later his brother, Emile, was to remember him also, among the lesser details of that return and the special green of the rushes under the rays of the setting sun.

Christian, seated on his father's shoulders, bore himself with the serene gravity of an Oriental potentate on the back of a sacred elephant.

His very light blue eyes seemed to see nothing, but all the family knew that three, or even six, months later Emile would suddenly tell the story of that day, with details that all the others had forgotten.

"At least give me your hat, or he'll ruin it."

It was like the movies. Mama entered the field of vision, raising one arm to take the straw hat; but she remained a vague figure, and Emile could not remember what dress she was wearing—a light one, surely, which she had probably made herself at home.

The little boy's attention was still concentrated on Father, who, now hatless, was holding one of Christian's round calves in each hand.

As for the latter, he was leaning on the scantily covered cranium of his father, and his head, which was very large, was swaying to the rhythm of his footsteps.

It did not matter much what time it was. It was the time of sunset, at last the time for sitting down and eating and drinking. Emile had said half an hour previously:

"I'm thirsty."

And the reply had been:

"You shall have a drink when we get to Pouilly."

He was always thirsty, and his parents would never stop to let him have a drink.

It was not only the hour of red sunset, of thirst and hunger, but also the hour of lassitude, feet stumbling in the dust of the road and the strange stale taste in the mouth. Even Mama, if she had spoken frankly, would have admitted that she was tired out.

But it would have been no use. The tall figure of Father, preceded by his great shadow, continued to walk with long strides, like a giant, with Christian balanced on his shoulders. He could walk like that for hours, doubtless for days, and Emile was convinced that he took no interest in the countryside.

He had decided on that particular Sunday:

"We'll go down by the Loire from Sancerre to Pouilly. We'll stop for the night at Pouilly, and tomorrow we'll do a little more walking."

He talked as though it were a treat! But it was only a treat for Father. That morning they had had to get dressed too early and run so as not to miss the train. They had eaten sandwiches at the water's edge, because of the excessive price charged at restaurants, and they had walked and walked, and Father, as he walked, his gaze fixed on the distance, wore an air of ecstasy, like that of a man who hears music, as though he were leading his family into some promised land.

"You're walking too fast, Father. Emile is out of breath."

Actually, it was Mama who was out of breath.

At last they arrived! Houses on the left, a real quay, and a bridge with numerous arches broke the monotony of that stretch of the Loire, which was scattered with sandbanks and small, overgrown islands.

The highway was not far off, and they heard the sound of traffic. They were now walking on a paved street.

"Well, won't you put Christian down now?"

Mama was always afraid of looking ridiculous, but Father maintained that children did not make anyone ridiculous.

They paused at the edge of the highway that runs through Pouilly, studying the terraces of hotels and restaurants.

The road was blue; the white houses reflected a bluish tint, but their awnings were striped with red and black, except one, a new one, which was a nice shade of orange.

"We could go home by bus," said Mama with a sigh, for hotels were expensive.

But no. It was Pentecost, and Father had decided to desert Nevers for two days.

Outside one of the hotels was a green-painted bench and green tubs planted with laurels. It was not too modern. It suited the style of the family, and Father crossed over to the sidewalk, relieved himself of Christian, whom he deposited on the bench, and then sat down beside him, exclaiming, "Ha!"

It was a "Ha" of happiness, the "Ha" of a man who has done his duty, achieved his purpose, and need be troubled by no misgivings.

"We'll first find out what it costs."

But of course! Naturally! While they waited, the rest of the family sat down on the straight-backed bench and watched the cars speed past, blowing their horns as they came to the turn.

"Two grenadines," said Father to the waitress, who was wearing a white apron. "And for you, Mama?"

"Nothing, thank you. We will be eating soon."

"Two grenadines and—wait—yes, a small Pernod."

He glanced apologetically at Mama. But it was Pentecost and he had carried Christian on his shoulders for more than four kilometers.

The rest was vague. Emile was not really sleepy, but his head was throbbing and his eyes were pricking because of the dust, and in spite of the grenadine there was still a stale taste in his mouth, the taste of summer Sundays when one walked forever through a motionless countryside.

There were a few people in the dining room, which had wallpaper with a floral decoration, mirrors, advertisements, and an old clock. All the tables were set for dinner, and in every glass there was a napkin folded to look like a fan.

The waitress who served them dinner was very young, and Emile paid no attention to her. But he seemed to remember much later, years and years later, that Mama had twice shrugged her shoulders.

4

Father was in a jolly mood, perhaps too jolly. He was not in the habit of drinking an apéritif. He was looking about him with the greedy eyes of a person who does not wish to miss any of the party.

"Where are you thinking of going tomorrow?"

"That depends. But we'll do at least ten kilometers."

One detail was important to Emile, although he alone was impressed by it. He saw a door open slightly and someone peered into the room. It was a cook, clad in white and wearing a tall hat. This was the first time the little boy had eaten a meal prepared by a cook, or at least the first time that he was aware of having done so.

"Shall I take the children up to bed?"

Emile grumbled on principle. He always grumbled when he was sent to bed. Nevertheless, he stumbled on the way upstairs. It was a white staircase, with a red carpet in the middle and a copper rod at every step. The house was old, with red tiles in the hallway and bedrooms. A window overlooking the street was open, and Mama shut it, cutting the three of them off from the sound of traffic.

Emile found himself in bed beside his brother, although it was still not quite dark, and he complained:

"Open the window."

His mother acquiesced. Once again they could hear the passing cars below and also the sound of voices, astonishingly clear, as they sometimes are on certain summer nights.

"You don't mind if I go downstairs for a little while? You will be good?"

The room was already heavy with sleep and the door closed silently.

The rest was a mingling of reality and dreams. Emile was vaguely aware of his father's voice coming from the terrace, but he could not see him seated under the moon while the pretty little waitress served him coffee.

Mama came downstairs at that moment and, after looking in the dining room, appeared at the front door.

"So there you are," she said.

"It's so warm. Are you going to have coffee?"

"Please."

"Are the children asleep?"

The little maid returned indoors, someone was calling to her:

"Rose!"

So her name was Rose. Mama sat down beside Father on the green bench, and they stayed there for perhaps an hour while darkness fell. Cars continued to pass, and now and then Emile had an anxious feeling that one of them would fly up through the window and crash on his bed.

He was awakened by a beam of light. Mama had returned to the bedroom next door and was undressing, leaving the door partly open.

"Thirsty," said Emile, to draw attention to himself.

"Why aren't you asleep?"

"I'm thirsty."

The face of Christian, laying beside him, was deeply flushed by the sun.

"Don't drink too fast."

"Where's Father?"

"He'll be up soon."

"What's he doing?"

Emile had a feeling that something was not quite right, but he did not worry about it.

"He's playing cards."

It was quite simple. Just when Maurice Arbelet was about to go upstairs with his wife, a plump, friendly, cheerful-looking man, who had evidently dined well, had approached him.

"Pardon, monsieur. Would you care to make a fourth?"

Father had glanced at Mama with that particular expression of his, such as when he had ordered the Pernod: a humble, apologetic gaze, which caused her to shrug her shoulders.

"If you want to."

"In that case . . . a limit of a thousand. No more."

Mme Arbelet was now in bed, and there were fewer cars on the road. Instead, one occasionally heard the clink of bottles and glasses down below, and the murmur of voices.

Arbelet was a little overexcited, because he had a guilty conscience. He should have been upstairs at the side of his wife. And he should not have accepted the liqueur offered him by one of his fellow players.

These were either bachelors or men who did not worry about their families. They were in the habit of spending their leisure time in cafés, drinking, playing cards, and eying the waitresses.

"I cut and lead the king of clubs. Your turn, monsieur."

The room was almost empty; there were no customers except themselves. It adjoined the restaurant, the quiet lounge of an old-fashioned café. The proprietor, still wearing his chef's hat, was standing behind the plumpest of the players, whom he seemed to know, and following the game.

"I play very rarely," stammered Arbelet, in apology for a mistake.

Through the open door of the restaurant Rose could be seen, clearing the tables. She surely was not more than sixteen years old.

Emile and Christian were both asleep. Mme Arbelet, eyes open, lay waiting, bathed in the dim light that came from outside.

They played a second game of a thousand points, and then, to finish off with, one of fifteen hundred points. At the end, the proprietor was seated behind Arbelet, on a chair turned back to front. There had already been two rounds of drinks when he offered a third, which it was impossible to refuse.

"Five hundred to nine!" Maurice Arbelet announced.

A moment before, Rose had entered the room to ask if she might go to bed, and Arbelet had had the impression that the proprietor had given her a little private nod. He was disturbed, excited by the thought that perhaps the man would later join the girl in her bedroom. He could not prevent himself from thinking about it, conjuring up precise pictures.

"Haven't you any more trumps?"

"Sorry. I've got the ten. Forgive me."

All the lights had been switched off except for two directly over the heads of the players.

"Well, there you are! You've won!"

He knew what had happened to him when he giggled, because he recognized that giggle.

"Let's hope my wife won't find out," he said to himself.

He climbed the stairs, clinging to the banister, and took pains not to mistake the door. In this he was successful, but then he knocked over a chair and nearly fell on top of it.

"Why don't you switch on the light?" asked a voice from the bed.

He realized that Mme Arbelet had not been asleep, that she was not even drowsy, but had her eyes wide open and all her wits about her.

"Because of the children."

"You know perfectly well they won't wake up."

He was careful not to let her see his face, because she would guess at once, although his clumsy entry had probably already enlightened her. She asked, although not in a tone of reproach:

"What have you been drinking?"

"A glass of marc. The proprietor offered one."

He got into bed, said good night, brushed her cheek with his lips, scarcely aware that he had forgotten to switch off the light and that his wife had to get up and do it.

Then there was a blankness, a hole crowded with unpleasant sensations, and shapeless dreams during which, two or three times, it seemed to him that his wife leaned over and forced him to turn onto his right side.

When he awoke, it was with a start, and he found himself sitting up in bed and then standing on the bedside rug.

"What's the matter?"

He could not speak. It would have been dangerous. He made a gesture indicating that his stomach was out of order, pulled on his jacket and trousers, and dashed into the hallway. He looked for some indication on the doors, but not finding what he sought, went hurriedly downstairs into the tiled passageway.

He heard a grunt, and a moment later bumped into something, which turned out to be a foot wearing a slipper, strangely situated at the height of his stomach.

He was bewildered. But then someone moved, a light was switched on, and he saw that a man was lying on a sofa against the wall of the passageway, his feet protruding over one arm.

"What d'you want?"

The man seemed already to have understood. He pointed to a door at the end of the passageway, which led to a yard. The whole scene was gray, lighted by the beams of a dirty electric bulb, which made everything look dusty.

"I—"

But Arbelet could not hold back long enough to reach the door. It was too late. He vomited on the floor, terrified that his wife would hear him.

Now that he had begun, and the mess would have to be cleaned up anyway, he might as well finish where he was. Between two hiccups, he found it necessary to apologize with a vague smile. He stammered:

"I don't know what was wrong with me."

He was clinging to a brass ball on the post at the foot of the stairs. There he was in darkness. The light shone only at the other end of the passageway, on the pink upholstered sofa, which served as a bed for the other man, who was now standing upright, looking larger than life.

Arbelet had twice glanced at him without really seeing him—that is, seeing only a thickset shadow, some sort of old worn garment, and the shapeless slippers of a sick person. Now that he was feeling better he turned his head to look straight at him.

"Might I have a glass of water?"

The man vanished into the darkness of the café. There was a clink of glasses and the running of a faucet. Then he returned to the light, and Arbelet stared at his face, at first without recognition. He gave himself time to take the glass and raise it to his lips before he began to shake with astonishment.

"Uncle Félix!"

The light seemed to irritate the big red-rimmed eyes, for the man made a grimace as he raised his head and looked at the speaker.

"It's you, is it?" was all he said. Then, while Arbelet was drinking, he went on, as a matter of form:

"What are you doing here?"

"I have been living in Nevers for the last three years."

"With your wife?"

The man was sleepy. He was very large, although his frame was not that of a strong man, but, rather, that of one who is swollen, bloated with soft fat or some other unhealthy substance, and he swayed as he stood, in a way that made one feel sick.

"And you?" asked Arbelet, without thinking.

"What about me?"

"Are you . . ."

As though it were necessary to ask! It was only necessary to look at the sofa and see the impress of a body. The person who had been lying there could be no one but the night porter. He had a beard several days old composed of gray hairs, stiff as thorns, and a head of hair that he must have cut himself, with clumsy swipes of the scissors.

"No need to say anything to Germaine," he murmured without conviction. "I'd just as soon not see her."

"But how long have you been—?"

The man cut him short with a gesture that implied, "What's the use? Don't let's waste time."

He was sleepy. He smelled of rancid sweat, of an unwashed human body. And he remembered that he was going to have to clean up the mess made by his niece's husband.

"Go on up!"

Arbelet went upstairs without finding anything else to say. He looked around once timidly and then re-entered the bedroom, now quite sober.

"Are you feeling better?" asked Germaine anxiously.

"Yes. It's all over."

11

"What was the trouble?"

Just at this moment Emile woke up, seeing light in his parents' room and his father's figure as it passed the bright rectangle of the open doorway.

"Nothing. Just a touch of indigestion."

"At least you haven't caught cold. Did you have to go outside?"

"No."

"Who were you talking to?"

Arbelet was taking his clothes off, while his son continued to listen without wanting to.

"Nobody. Well, that's to say, to the night porter."

"You sound rather queer."

"Me?"

"Not so loud. You'll wake up the children."

They fell to whispering. But, curiously enough, Emile heard them better than when they were talking in undertones, despite the hiss at the ends of the words.

"It will be better if you don't see him."

"Who?"

"Your Uncle Félix. He's the person downstairs."

"You mean the night porter? What did he say to you?"

"Nothing. He . . ."

The lamp was switched off, but the parents' bedroom was still dimly illuminated by light from outside.

"He knows that I'm here?"

"Yes."

"He didn't ask to see me?"

There were long silences, during which nothing was to be heard but the regular breathing of Christian.

"I was so embarrassed! And now I've just thought of something. It was he who . . ."

"Who did what?"

"Who will have to . . . Listen, Germaine. I didn't have

time to reach the yard. So that it's your Uncle Félix who will be obliged to . . ."

There was a movement and a creak of bedsprings.

"I think I ought to go down."

"Look, Maurice. Have you any money on you?"

"About three hundred francs."

"There are two hundred in my bag, on the mantelpiece. I'm wondering if you ought to . . ."

Emile heard the click of the fastening of his mother's handbag. Then he dropped off to sleep again, and when next he opened his eyes, the roar of traffic, accompanied by sunshine, was flooding through the wide-open windows.

2

The encounter with Arbelet had in no way changed the course of Félix's night or altered his mood. He had gone to the closet where the brooms and rags were kept and then, without hurrying, he had cleaned up the passageway, grunting as he did so:

"Shit!"

But he was not referring to Arbelet's vomit or to any particular person. Indeed, when he talked to himself, as he often did, it was in brief phrases or single words, mumbled so that they were unrecognizable; he never made direct reference to any particular person or thing.

He said, "Shit!" and to understand this one needed to be the man himself, to have lived the life he had lived, to be a night porter, sick or rotting in every part of his body, smelling unpleasant to the point where he was conscious of the fact, and to wonder, whenever he lay down to rest, whether his carcass would agree to get up in the morning.

"Shit!"

This was directed at no one special and perhaps not even at people in general. Perhaps the word simply referred to Félix himself, what he was and everything that had happened to him. Luck! Or fate! Or else . . .

Quite often, indeed almost every night, particularly when late-arriving customers aroused him after his first slumber, he grunted:

"I'll have to kill one."

The proprietor had heard him say this several times. So had Thérèse and little Rose. He made no secret of it. He was not joking. He said it while he went about his duties, and he was convinced that one day it would happen.

Meanwhile, having finished cleaning up, he went into the café to look at a black-rimmed clock by means of his pocket flashlight.

The time was ten to one. But the clock face, its two hands set at the appropriate angle, did not have the same meaning for him as it had for other people.

Ten to one meant that it was not worthwhile going back to rest on the sofa in the passageway. A new period of the night was beginning, when there was no likelihood of the arrival of customers.

Nevertheless, to guard against the improbability, Félix opened the door at the end that led to the yard. As always when he opened that door, he encountered a gust of cold, damp air and, over to the right, the light rattle of a chain, as the dog moved in its kennel.

Félix lighted a pipe. Sometimes, looking up, he could see a lighted window—a customer who was feeling unwell, or one who could not get to sleep and was reading.

It was no business of his. He crossed the yard to the former stables, now converted into a garage. By the door he found an old pair of rubber boots, which he had patched with strips of inner tube. He pulled the switch, and a twenty-five-watt bulb, a single one, glowed in the wide extent of darkness.

The dog had settled down again in its kennel. Félix moved slowly, partly because there was no point in hurrying, but also because everything in him felt more or less ill.

He approached one of the objects aligned in the half-darkness. They were cars, mostly standard models, but occasionally there was a really good one. The way he tackled his next duty depended on the number he had to wash, one or two or three. The water was icy, even in summer.

A hose had been installed, but it was a garden hose, not really powerful enough to wash the mud off the body and, particularly, the wheels.

"I'll damn well have to kill one."

He said this while he was working and, as it happened, he made a grammatical error, using the masculine form *un* for the word *one;* but in the French language cars, like women, are feminine. He repeated the words, this time correcting the gender.

Actually, he was not thinking of any woman, but of cars in general. Beastly objects, full of dirty corners, and with smooth surfaces on which the sponge left smears if they were not sufficiently rinsed—dirty beasts with hard, spiky skins expressly designed to take the skin off one's fingers.

He must not forget to remove all the cigarette butts from the inside. Because customers never left the key in the ignition, he had to push the cars, steering them by reaching the wheel through the open window.

Shit, that's what it was! All ot it! If there were only two cars to be washed, he would be finished by four in the morning, at the time the first trucks could be heard on their way to the market at Nevers. Félix selected one of the cars he had just washed, the largest of them, and stretched out on the back seat, where he could sleep for an hour and a half.

Well, it was his niece's husband's business, and nothing to do with him. The fact is that he had scarcely given the matter a thought, except for an instant, to picture his niece upstairs in bed, and that had been automatic.

Now it was daylight, and the dog in the yard was tugging at its chain. Félix got painfully out of the car and went into the café.

Everything was timed to the minute. That was still the

best thing in life. One knew where one was going and what to expect around every corner.

Behind the counter he had a small gas stove, with a red rubber tube attached. One caught the smell of gas for some moments, and then the stove burst into flame, always with the same plop, while Félix was filling a saucepan at the faucet.

He had no need to listen for the stove. Probably no one else would have heard it. But, decayed though he was, he could have heard the scuttling of a rat at the other end of the house.

It was of interest to no one, but that is how he was made. And while he listened he saw, or as good as saw. For instance, on the next floor, three rooms away, just above the hanging lamp in the dining room, the proprietor was getting up. The lamp trembled slightly, so slightly that no one who did not know would notice it. Nevertheless, it trembled.

The proprietor could very well have stayed in bed later. He did not go to market. Meat, fish, and vegetables were all delivered to the hotel. As for the coffee for guests who left before eight, this was heated on Félix's stove.

However, the proprietor got up. He had not wanted to. He was sleepy. He was always sleepy, all day long, always tired, and had a grayish tint, shadows under his eyes, and no appetite.

He took care as he rose to do so silently, in order not to awaken his wife. He pulled on his trousers, tucked his nightshirt into them, stepped into a pair of slippers, and hurried out into the hallway.

This was because of Rose. If Rose had not been there, it would have been some other girl. The truth was that during the day he waited for the moment when Thérèse, who was not pretty and who always had her five-year-old boy

17

clinging to her skirt, went down into the cellar, at which point he hurried after Rose.

Félix knew everything, everything that happened in the house. Everything that everyone did, and even how they washed!

He allowed himself just enough time to swallow the coffee he had made, with three lumps of sugar; and also time to hear, or, rather, to guess, that in the attic on the top floor at the other end of the house Thérèse's alarm clock was ringing.

He crossed the yard and entered the garage, which was nearly as dark as it was at night, illuminated only by a rectangle of glass in the door. Inside were poultry, tools, packing cases, and barrels. At the height of what would normally have been an upper floor there was a sort of gallery, reached by way of a ladder. At a certain point on this gallery were sacks and a cistern, forming a barrier and preventing anyone down below from seeing an iron bedstead and a jug. This was Félix's bedroom.

Quite often during the day, customers came to discuss their business in the garage, not knowing that they could be overheard. They never guessed that the old man was lying just above them and only had to raise his head to see them through the chinks between the sacks.

But this was not all. There were two packing cases standing one on top of the other, and Félix now climbed onto them. Perhaps one day he would tumble off that rickety scaffolding and break his neck among the cars. Meanwhile, he scrambled up every morning to the topmost case, and in doing so came to a dormer window in the roof, which must have been several centuries old and must have served to illumine God knew what. Had not someone maintained that in the old days the garage had been the most important part of the house? Just opposite him was Rose's window, and since it looked out onto nothing but the roof, it was without a curtain. Generally the window was open, and if his spy hole had not been glassed in, Félix would have heard everything.

The same comedy had been enacted every time during the three months that had passed since it first took place. Previously the room had been occupied by Thérèse, and with her everything had been quite different, because she was practiced in vice.

Then Rose had been engaged. At first the proprietor, Monsieur Jean, as he was called, had hovered around her with self-conscious laughter, devising pretexts to get her alone in a corner. He had even gone so far as to teach her to polish shoes, because this work was done in the laundry.

One morning Félix had seen him enter her room when she was wearing nothing but a pair of panties, and she had held up her face towel to cover her breasts. Now she pretended to be asleep right up to the last moment. Five minutes later it was over and the proprietor usually left. Then, as though he needed to get his breath, he could be seen down below and could be heard coming and going, fiddling with the stove, opening shutters, peering through the windows at the yard.

As for Félix, he remained at his post, watching Rose while she casually dressed.

"Nothing but . . . !"

No. On these occasions he was more likely to say, "I'll have to kill one." Why not, "The day I can get hold of a woman"?

No one knew that he was there. No one knew what he was really like. All of them, whoever they were, including the proprietress, Mme Fernand, who occupied a room two windows away, went about their business without suspecting that he was spying on their privacy!

It was still not time for Mme Fernand. She rose later, after eight, and her toilet lasted anything up to two hours, including an hour devoted simply to her hair and her fingernails.

Thus, the proprietor had three women, without counting the casuals he met on his visits to Nevers or La Charté.

"What are you doing up there?"

He nearly fell off his perch, not from fright, but because he was startled. There was nothing to be afraid of. It was Thérèse, a girl of twenty-four who already looked faded. She was blowzy and vicious. She had a husband, a Pole who worked at the quarry at Tracy, fifteen kilometers away, and who came to see her only when he was drunk.

"Let me have a look, you dirty old man."

Without waiting for him to make room for her, she climbed up beside him, stared, and exclaimed:

"Well I never!"

The proprietor was still in Rose's room, and Thérèse remarked:

"He just has to have it all day long! ... What am I supposed to be doing here? Oh, yes, number 3 is leaving and wants his tank filled."

Thus, minute by minute and action by action, the house had sprung to life and the day had got into gear, under a sun that was already high and hot, dispelling the mists that rose from the Loire and drying the damp patches on the road left from the night.

"Have you ordered breakfast?"

Maurice Arbelet was nearly ready. He was standing in

front of the open window while his wife dressed Christian, who, as he did every morning, took the better part of half an hour to wake up.

"Do you think we need breakfast?"

"Money again!"

Emile hurriedly asserted, "I'm hungry," and his mother replied, "We'll buy some croissants at the bakery and eat them on our way."

After all, why waste six francs on a breakfast consisting of coffee and two croissants?

"Don't you think the children are too tired to go on walking?"

The one who was tired was Arbelet himself, but he dared not say so. He had a dizzy feeling and there was a slightly painful throbbing at his temples.

They could hear Thérèse tidying up the terrace and flinging buckets of water over the sidewalk. Some people were talking loudly in a doorway. The day was still almost new.

"We might as well do at least a few kilometers. We can stop a bus whenever we like."

Mama was rinsing the toothbrushes, wrapping the soap in a piece of paper, folding a towel, and putting everything in the large handbag that was used on these excursions. She overlooked a comb, but remembered it in time. Arbelet said:

"I'll go on down."

Emile of course at once cried, "Me, too!"

"You're to stay with me," ordered his mother, thinking of Uncle Félix. Her husband, who was also thinking of him, gave her a look of understanding.

Was it better to see her uncle again or not? In any event, the children must not be allowed to know that a member of the family had fallen so low in the social scale.

The first person Arbelet encountered on the stairs was Rose, who was in a hurry and smelled of soap.

"Pardon, monsieur."

"Not at all."

She was running, dancing down the stairway three steps at a time. She was barely sixteen!

"Hurry up and serve the breakfast for 6 and 7," the proprietor called to her as she entered the café.

This meant the Arbelet family, and Maurice stopped him.

"Don't bother. We aren't having breakfast."

"Not even coffee?"

"No. We never drink it as early as this."

Arbelet blushed, and was annoyed at himself for blushing, every time there was any question of money.

"Will you let me have the bill?"

"That won't take long. Forty and thirty; seventy francs."

Naturally it was more than Arbelet had expected. It always was!

"There were the drinks yesterday evening. You stood a round, didn't you? Plus a glass of wine, two grenadines, and an apéritif." Mama was now coming down, and Arbelet hastily paid, especially since the proprietor said no more.

He heard the gasoline pump working in the yard but did not know it was being operated by Uncle Félix. Another customer came down, one of the cardplayers of the previous evening, and perhaps he, too, was going to talk about the round of drinks.

"We're on our way," announced Mama, which meant at that moment, "I'm going to the bakery with the children to buy croissants."

"That's good. I'm just waiting for my change and then I'll follow you." He badly wanted a cup of coffee. It was ridiculous to feel so acute a need, and even more so to let it weigh on his conscience, but that is how it was. He looked at Rose, and already had a guilty feeling because of the way he looked at her.

"Mademoiselle, would you mind bringing me a cup of coffee."

He could see his family, with Mama holding both children by the hand while they crossed the road. One might think that nature itself was perspiring, and that the town exuded a scent of summer; and when Rose bent over him as she served the coffee, he was surprised to be able to distinguish her own particular smell from that of all the other smells of the morning.

"Laced?"

He did not understand at first.

"No, thank you, just a lump of sugar."

Why did he keep looking through the open doorway? Why was he not at ease with his conscience? It was not because of his wife's uncle; nor was it particularly because of the card game and the three glasses of marc.

He looked into the kitchen and saw, seated in a corner, an old fat woman peeling vegetables. Outside, Thérèse, bent double, was wiping the edge of the sidewalk with a damp cloth, her skirt rising as she did so to disclose her bare legs.

The proprietor, at the counter, was dreamily regarding a menu he had not yet drawn up, and Arbelet reflected with amazement that he was not yet thirty-two years old. Why should he be amazed? What was so extraordinary about this place? In what way was the life of the proprietor of the White Horse Inn more enviable than the life of anyone else?

"Rose! Have a look in the refrigerator and see if there's any chicken left."

The Arbelets had no refrigerator, but they had decided to buy one. They rarely ate chicken. In their house there were no doors open to all manner of surprises, or a yard that resounded with the engine of a car, or a highway and a grocery store opposite, or laurels in tubs painted green. . . .

And there were no . . .

He gave a ten-franc tip, and was angry with himself for doing so, because he would not dare tell his wife. He had heard the shop bell ring a hundred yards down the street, that of the bakery his family had just entered.

He drank his coffee with a sense of shame. He would have liked to stay longer, for no reason; but he dragged himself away from the White Horse and strode briskly down the street in time to see the shopkeeper plunge her hand into a large jar to get out some red-and-white candies, which Christian had probably asked for. Mama was carefully counting the money, placing each piece separately on the marble counter. As she left the shop, Arbelet heard her say:

"Not in the street. It's not polite."

They had to wait till they had left the town before eating the croissants. One thing was quite certain: they would be thirsty, particularly Emile, who was always thirsty.

"At the next village," Mama promised, and every hundred yards the little boy repeated, "Is it far?"

"Keep your eyes on the road."

Was it the familiar phrase that aroused in Arbelet an irresistible desire to turn back? Was his sense of guilt so strong that he felt compelled to say, "I tried to get hold of him"?

"Did you see him?"

"No. But we shall have to do something."

"Don't you think we've done enough already?"

Christian's head, that big head on a small, tightly clad body, was already rocking as he stared too far ahead of him past the things that were immediately visible. Emile was kicking a stone along, surprised that he had not yet been told that he was wearing out his shoes.

"We really can't leave him in a situation like that," Father said.

"But whose fault is it?" answered Mama.

Then, as Emile looked up, she added hastily:

"But don't let's talk about it now."

"Who is it, Mama?"

"Who?"

"The man who is in the situation . . ."

They turned to the right and, leaving the highway, followed a road that led to the bank of the Loire.

"Give them their croissants."

There were still drops of dew on the weeds growing on the bank, and the ground, encrusted with dried mud, still bore traces of the hoof marks of a herd of cows. Mama sighed, as she always did, and said:

"How good it smells!"

And once again Arbelet was on the point of turning back. He was feeling sad, or, rather, peevish. A bit of both, with also a twinge of disquiet. . . .

Mme Fernand, the proprietress of the White Horse Inn, who was a good-looking woman of thirty with a well-rounded figure and soft, regular features, had just opened her window to let in the morning sun, and countless specks of dust has risen from the bed to rejoin the flow of nature. A few yards away were the old tiles of the garage roof, in which there was a dirt-encrusted window to which no one had ever paid any attention.

Only at about ten, when Mme Fernand had gone down to her cash desk, did old Félix stretch himself out on his iron bedstead and, indifferent to the sounds and sights of the house, sink into the heavy slumber of a sick animal.

"Don't you want it?" asked Mme Arbelet, offering her husband the last croissant.

She divided it between the two children.

3

One did not precisely know anything. But was there really anything to know? One caught snatches of conversation here and there, hints of events that had still not taken place but were nonetheless part of the future. Threads were interwoven, that was all. Yet not even that. They were like tangled string, the threads of several destinies, three, four, or perhaps more, with nothing to show that they would form themselves into a knot.

Nine started work. She was seated in a corner of the kitchen near the window, from which she did not move from morning till night. As was her habit, she collected the peelings in her blue linen apron, and a half-filled bucket of water, between her slippers, awaited the potatoes. As in a Dutch painting, the light that slanted in through the window illumined nothing but her, leaving the rest of the kitchen in half-darkness.

Who else was there at that moment and exactly what time was it? It was a Thursday, because Thérèse's child was not at school but was loitering in the yard wondering what mischief he could get into.

It was not yet ten. In the yard the air was motionless, almost sticky. The gasoline pump, exposed to the full light of the sun, was painted blood red. One after another Nine's potatoes dropped into the bucket, causing occasional drops of water to splash out.

"What happened this morning?"

Thérèse was there, engaged in some dirty job, because she had her sleeves rolled up and there was a black mark on her face. The proprietor was also there, getting things out of the refrigerator.

When Nine spoke she never seemed to address anyone in particular or to expect a reply. She uttered the words without moving, to relieve herself of some idea that was occupying her thoughts. Once the idea was out, it was over and it did not matter whether anyone picked it up.

"It was a young couple," replied Thérèse in a sulky voice.

The proprietor asked suspiciously:

"What happened to the young couple?"

It all amounted to nothing, less than nothing. During the forty years that she had been there, peeling vegetables, seated in that same corner, where dropsy had gradually caused her to swell, Nine had acquired the right, after an hour's silence, to launch a sentence into the air, and Thérèse had the right to answer. And the proprietor had the right to ask what it was all about.

"They wanted to be awakened at four in the morning to go fishing," grunted Thérèse.

Monsieur Jean gave her a brief angry look, because he did not like to hear anyone who seemed to be complaining.

"What does that matter to you? Was it you who had to wake them up?"

"No. Félix."

"Well then?"

"Well nothing . . ."

Nevertheless, it was the kind of morning that a child lives through only a few times, but that by some miracle remains fixed in its memory like a summing up of summer.

Henri, Thérèse's small son, dressed in red-checked overalls that had become too small for him, was amusing himself by kicking pebbles about, keeping his hands in his pockets.

Nine's lips were pouted as though in a smile. No one knew for certain whether it was really a smile or just a particular shape of her mouth. She was so unlike other people that no one tried to relate her expressions to those of ordinary mortals.

She was Nine! A being always exactly like herself. Had she been different when she had first arrived, in the days of Mme Fernand's grandfather? She had been as fat and flabby, and she had difficulty in walking, so she was never made to wait on tables. Where did she come from? From what village? No one knew. Nor was it of any importance. She had seated herself and she had stayed.

What was most extraordinary was that one day she had given birth to a child, not that anyone had any knowledge of a man in her life. It is true that the child had died at birth. . . .

"Down she comes!"

No need to ask if Thérèse had any affection for Mme Fernand. It was sufficient to hear the tone in which she spoke those words, which was so obvious that Monsieur Jean picked her up on it.

"Couldn't you speak more civilly?"

"What have I said wrong?"

The day had got off to a bad start. Mme Fernand was now downstairs, but she went straight to her cash desk without passing through the kitchen. She could be heard speaking to Rose, who was setting the tables in the dining room.

"That young married couple haven't got back yet?"

Again Monsieur Jean encountered Thérèse's eyes, and for no reason he felt furiously angry with her. Was it because her hair was in disorder and because she had a general look of being unwashed? Or because she always behaved as though she were being victimized?

"What's wrong with you?"

"Nothing."

He was preparing a dish of ravioli, rolling out the dough on the wooden table. His wife called to him:

"Jean!"

"Just a minute!"

As though by accident, he once again encountered the gaze of the maid-of-all-work. Nevertheless, he finished rolling the dough, wiped his fingers on his apron, and went up the stone steps into the dining room.

At this time of day it was on the sunny side of the house. Coming from the kitchen was like coming out of a cellar. All the white tablecloths shown with light, and through the open door one could see the road, the laurels, and the green bench.

"How much have you taken?"

Mme Fernand, hair immaculate, quiet-mannered and serene, had arranged the contents of the cashbox in a series of piles in front of her. Pencil in hand, she now sat waiting.

"This morning?" asked Monsieur Jean, who, in spite of himself, had a guilty look. He was always guilty of something or other where she was concerned.

"Yes. Has someone brought in a bill?"

"I don't think so. Why do you ask?"

"Because there are three hundred francs missing."

Decidedly this was a bad day! Monsieur Jean should have given himself time to think. Instead, he said foolishly:

"Oh, yes. I gave the butcher some money."

"Have you his bill?"

"No. He just wanted some cash. I gave him three hundred francs."

Trifles, nothing but trifles! He now remembered that earlier that morning, when he was having his breakfast, Thérèse had come to him asking for money. What exactly had she said? He had forgotten. He had been thinking of something else. Anyway, he hadn't given her any.

Now he would have to warn the butcher, so that he would not give the show away.

"Have you done the menu?"

"It's already been put up."

He never spoke to his wife first thing in the morning, because she was still asleep, and when she came downstairs, they both behaved as though they were seeing each other for the first time.

"I must get on with my ravioli."

But he was not able to do so immediately. Returning to the kitchen, he noticed that Thérèse was no longer there and asked, "Where is she?"

Nine, without speaking, nodded in the direction of the window. Thérèse was crossing the yard in the direction of the cellar, where every morning she filled the half-bottles of white wine that were placed on all the tables in the dining room. Since this took her past her son, she evidently took advantage of the fact to shake him and send him to play elsewhere, because he went off in the direction of the yard gate.

Monsieur Jean crossed the yard in his turn, and when, shortly afterward, Rose entered the kitchen, she exclaimed in astonishment:

"No one here?"

Old Nine repeated the motion of her head toward the empty yard. But it was no longer empty. Félix had emerged from the garage, his hair in disorder and with the sulky look on his face he always wore when he had just got up. Presumably he heard sounds coming from the cellar, for he looked in that direction and paused to listen.

The fact of living together makes guesswork easy. But Rose, who know nothing, asked:

"What's happening?"

Nine did not answer, having nothing to say. Mme Fernand was still seated at her cash desk, making twenty copies of the menu, one for each table. Rose should have been on her way upstairs to change her apron and wash her hands again before serving.

Félix came tottering across the yard, still listening, and as he opened the kitchen door the sound of voices was to be heard coming from the cellar.

"Shit!"

He was bound to repeat the word, or he would not have been himself. And he wore an air of disgust.

This did not prevent him from opening the refrigerator and groping inside it with hands that were deliberately unwashed. He made a point, for example, of fishing for anchovies, where they lay in a bowl of dressing, eating some, and then putting his greasy fingers back into the bowl.

Rose had seen him do it so often that she said nothing. She saw Monsieur Jean come striding out of the cellar with a furious look on his face. But after covering a short distance, with his rage still upon him, he turned back to the half-open door, and in a moment was to be seen gesticulating in the shadows of the cellar. One seemed to hear the sound of a cry.

At this moment the occupants of the cellar turned their heads, for Mme Fernand was standing in the doorway. She asked calmly:

"What's going on?"

"Nothing, madame."

"Tell me, Félix, what did you serve that young married couple this morning?"

"Coffee with milk, bread and butter."

"They didn't have anything else before they left?"

She watched her husband as he again left the cellar, this time for good, and crossed the sun-filled rectangle of the yard, but she took no further notice of him and returned to her cash desk.

Félix, still on his feet, was continuing to eat. He always fed himself in this fashion, on anything he could find in the refrigerator, and everyone had grown so used to it that no place was ever set for him at any table, nor was he summoned to any meal.

Monsieur Jean's first impulse, when he returned to the kitchen, was to get back to his ravioli, but he instinctively glanced into the dining room, where he saw the butcher leaning against the cash desk.

Oh, well! What could he do about it? It was better to get on with his work while he waited to see how things would turn out.

Oddly enough, to relieve his nerves, he addressed to Félix the same question his wife had.

"What did you serve them this morning?"

The young married couple, who had a passion for fishing, had been for the past four hours tucked away amid the reeds on the bank of the Loire.

To all appearances life went on as it did every day in all the hotels bordering the highways. To be conscious of anything unusual one needed to have a thorough inside knowledge of the business. The moment the front door opened, or a car pulled up outside, all faces changed their expression, except that of Mme Fernand, who had no need to do so, for she bore as usual her placid, everyday face.

She had said nothing, either about the butcher or about the three hundred francs. She rose to her feet when necessary and welcomed customers with a friendly smile.

"There are three of you? You'd like to be near a window? Rose! A table for three here. Will you have the twenty-five-franc lunch or the one for eighteen francs?"

The air was beginning to smell of gasoline. In the kitchen, lard or butter spluttered and there was a glow of flames whenever anyone moved a saucepan on the stove. Monsieur Jean, with a stony countenance, was dealing out portions.

Rose had still not understood. All she knew was that when she left the cellar, Thérèse had gone straight up to her room, and that she had had to go after her. She had talked to her through the door.

"Monsieur Jean says you're to come down right away."

"To hell with him!"

"At least fifteen customers have arrived."

"I don't give a damn!"

"Open the door!"

"I won't!"

A little later Mme Fernand, seeing that Rose was serving all the tables by herself, asked, without moving from her place:

"Isn't Thérèse here?"

"She's just coming down."

She came down with reddened eyes, too much powder and rouge on her cheeks, and lips so brightly painted that the lipstick seemed to have melted. It was also noticeable that she had a bruise near her temple, and Rose glanced at Monsieur Jean with a certain amount of alarm.

When Félix had finished his meal, he went back to bed,

as usual, because he did not have to clean out the yard until three.

"Two *quenelles!*"

Mme Fernand noted every item on small slips of paper, while keeping an eye on the tables where every day a new set of people ate the same *quenelles,* made almost the same remarks, and asked the same questions. Through the open windows she saw the return of the young married couple, loaded with their fishing gear. They went to wash in the lavatory off the passageway.

Since they had been there two days, these two had already become friendly with the household. The young man went up to the cash desk.

"What are you giving us to eat today? We're both starving."

"Have you ordered anything special?"

And Mme Fernand called:

"Jean!"

"Yes?"

Although she was now calling to the kitchen, she did not lose sight of the café. Hearing a noise, she said to Thérèse:

"Go and see what's happening."

An outburst of voices followed a moment later. Then there was a silence and a further outburst. Customers stopped eating to listen.

Thérèse did not come back. There was the sound of a glass being smashed to bits. Rose went to the open door, and Mme Fernand glanced inquiringly at at her.

"What is it?"

Rose approached and murmured to her:

"It's her husband. He's drunk."

The people at lunch were continuing with their meal. Mme Fernand called to Jean:

"Thérèse's husband is here."

"Where?"

"In the café."

He ran there, because it was necessary. Once inside, he closed the door behind him. Mme Fernand returned to her seat. Rose had to hurry from table to table. And now there was a fresh sound of breaking glass, but this time it was a pane in one of the front windows. A man with a strong Polish accent was shouting at the top of his voice. Then the front door opened, and Monsieur Jean thrust in front of him a reeling drunkard, who, going backward down the steps, very nearly fell on his back.

People smiled. They smiled even more when they saw the Pole install himself on the sidewalk opposite and, with gesticulations, bellow a string of threats, which to them were incomprehensible.

Monsieur Jean returned to his kitchen, and his wife asked him:

"Shall I telephone the police?"

"If you want to."

The incident had happened before, although with less violence. About once a fortnight, Stephan came over from the quarry, already half drunk, demanded money from his wife, and went to spend it in all the drinking places in Pouilly, until, having had all he could take, he came to make trouble at the White Horse Inn.

"Hello! Yes, this is the White Horse."

She was speaking in a low voice, with one hand cupping the mouthpiece of the telephone, while she kept an eye on the customers.

In the kitchen Monsieur Jean tied a handkerchief around his hand, which had been cut by a fragment of glass, and went on with his cooking. Thérèse took advantage of the fact that she had to fetch a dish from the kitchen to murmur:

"I warned you."

They did not hide anything from Nine. In fact, they did not hide anything from anyone except Mme Fernand.

"The boy told him everything."

Monsieur Jean went on loading dishes and plates with portions of stew and cutting up beefsteaks.

As though he guessed what he was in for, the Pole gradually withdrew, walking backward, shouting threats and insults, until, after a short time, he found himself held up by a sergeant and a policeman.

"You're coming with us, my boy."

There was an argument. And then the Pole, still gesticulating, was seen to accompany the two uniformed men.

Filter coffee pots were already being placed on the tables, and Mme Fernand arose to go around with a big bottle of marc, which she always served herself. The bus from Nevers stopped thirty yards away. Two local women, dressed in black, got out, and then, just as it was about to move off, a man emerged of whom no one took any notice.

It was Maurice Arbelet, who had asked to have the afternoon off and had lunched early.

He was not recognized, even when he entered the dining room. Only Rose raised her eyebrows, thinking that she had seen him somewhere before, while, smiling, he looked around for a place.

"Have you come for lunch?"

"No, thank you. I've had lunch. I'd just like coffee."

Thérèse's small son was out on the bank of the river, enviously watching a boy of his own age who was fishing and had already caught two small fish. With his slightly twisted legs, overlarge knees, hands in his pockets, and his head a little on one side, he had a crafty look.

"Tell me, mademoiselle . . . "

Arbelet was in luck. He was being served by Rose, and both were in the sunshine.

"The night porter—is he here at present?"

"He's asleep."

"In the house?"

"Above the garage. If you like, I'll send someone to fetch him. That is, if you wouldn't mind waiting a moment while I give number 4 their bill."

It was the day when Mme Arbelet and the children had lunch with her mother.

"You know it's no use giving him money," Germaine had said, referring to her uncle. "He gets rid of it in a few days."

Even if there was no one there, if the children were out of earshot, they never referred to Uncle Félix except in an undertone.

"It's not so much to give him money. . . ."

"Well, what do you want to do?"

"I don't know. Just talk to him. Find out if we might not help him in some other way. If, for example, he might go into an old people's home. After all, he's your mother's brother."

The White Horse in the sunshine—filled with the clatter of forks and the scent of coffee and marc, beside the smooth highway along which cars sped, but notable above all for the black dresses of Thérèse and Rose, and their little bright-white aprons, and the indulgent smile of Mme Fernand, who seemed to be protecting all her people—the White Horse was a place so marvelous that Arbelet, while he sugared his coffee, of which the metal lid had burned his fingers, would have liked time to stand still.

He lit a cigarette, and found that it tasted different from the way it did in other places.

He could not know that the Pole, having been solidly knocked about, was now being thrust toward the door of the police station and released with the following words of parting:

"If you're still in Pouilly an hour from now, you'll get some more and you'll sleep in a cell."

Uncle Félix awoke, saw from the sun that it was still not time for him to go back to work, and stayed where he was, open eyed, sniffing his old man's smell.

4

He had asked politely at the cash desk:

"Will it be all right for me to go and have a word with Monsieur Drouin?"

Mme Fernand had blinked for a moment, because the name Drouin meant nothing to her, but then she had understood.

"Of course. Go through the kitchen. When you get to the garage, you will have to shout very loud, because he's hard of hearing."

She did not in the least concern herself with why he wanted to see the night porter, as Arbelet had expected her to. In the doorway of the kitchen, he met Rose, who was coming out with a tray, and he stood aside, but not enough, so that he brushed against her. Blundering into the kitchen, where there were only the proprietor and Nine, he stammered, from force of habit, "I beg your pardon."

Monsieur Jean, who was drinking strong coffee, saw him go by without even reflecting that a customer was passing through the kitchen to go to the garage. He was absorbed by his own thoughts, into which Arbelet had intruded only as a furtive shadow.

"Turn it the other way," said Nine, seeing Arbelet trying to turn the door handle in the wrong direction.

What did it matter if they thought him shy or nervous? That was not the case, but he always had a feeling of awkwardness when he found himself among strangers.

He was not at home in this place, and never would be.

He vividly perceived that the White Horse Inn formed a whole in itself, a separate world, which was self-sufficient, with its sun, its joys, its smells, its dramas, and even its own language. That, incidentally, was why, as he crossed the kitchen, he had glanced sidelong at the proprietor, wondering if he was the master of a small universe or if it was Mme Fernand, passive and dignified at her desk.

He jumped, because the dog emerged ferociously from its kennel; but the chain was too short.

"Monsieur Drouin!" he called, taking a step into the garage. "Monsieur Drouin!"

There was no reply, and he advanced farther, changing his form of address.

"Monsieur Félix! Monsieur Félix!"

The man above, lying on his mattress, had his eyes wide open. The name Drouin had astonished him, chiefly because he had not recognized Arbelet's voice, and so he waited. He waited until either the intruder gave up and went away or he himself would be moved to get up and go down.

"Hello! Is there anyone there?"

Félix did not smile, even though he noted that the intruder was losing his self-possession. His only reaction, after a few moments, was to say, in a toneless voice, like someone uttering a phrase of conventional politeness:

"Just the same I'll have to kill one."

He had risen. Arbelet, looking up, called:

"Is that you, Uncle?"

Seen from below, the old man presented a monstrous appearance. Since the low bed could not be seen, it was difficult to understand where the dark, slowly rising mass was coming from, or even to realize at first that its shape was due to the ragged blanket draped over the night porter's shoulders. One had the impression of a living heap emerging from a world of dust, and Félix's hoarse voice added to the strangeness of the scene.

"It's you, is it? What do you want?"

"I just want to talk to you for a minute."

Félix clambered down the ladder. He had hesitated, but then he had reflected that it was only a few minutes until the time when he would have to go back to work. His passing aroused a hen, which fled away squawking.

"What do you want?" he repeated.

Looking at him, Arbelet recalled something that Thérèse had said to Félix that morning when he was at the desk paying his bill. Félix had come into the kitchen, walking bandy-legged and dragging his feet, with his head seeming to hang from his shoulders. He was sniffing loudly instead of using a handkerchief, and his eyes were as watery as the drippings from his nose. She had burst out at him:

"You damn well know you do it on purpose!"

She herself had an uncle with a passion for frightening children, who had caused one of her girl cousins to contract jaundice!

Félix, indeed, deliberately behaved disgustingly. When he scratched himself, he did so slowly and with a persistence that made one feel physically unwell.

"Listen, Uncle. Germaine and I have had a long talk about you."

They were both standing, Félix half in the sunlight, with a wisp of straw clinging to the hairs of his beard, and Arbelet in the shade. The dog, with its muzzle thrust outside the kennel, lay watching them and wanting to bark.

"Why are you now living in Nevers?"

Arbelet had nothing to hide, and nothing with which to reproach himself. If he had left Orléans, where he had

42

worked for the Water Company, and transferred to Nevers, where he had found a roughly equivalent job, it had been in order to be nearer to his mother-in-law when she lost her husband. Why then should he be the one who seemed embarrassed as he stammered:

"Listen, Uncle!"

Any policeman, encountering Félix in the street, would have taken him along to the police station, kicking him in the calves of his legs. And yet, once he had got him there, and stood face to face with him, he would perhaps have been the more ill at ease of the two!

Why?

And why should Monsieur Jean, who addressed everyone as *tu,* quite often say *vous* to the night porter when they were alone together?

He was dirty! He was repugnant! He coughed and scratched with a pleasure from sickening other people, and yet no one could sustain his heavy gaze, or face those red-rimmed eyes.

"What it comes to is that we think this is not the right place for you. You can't stay much longer in this situation."

"You think not?"

Was he threatening or only being sarcastic? There were moments when one wondered if the whole thing were not an act and if, with a smile, he would rid himself of his vermin and his resentments, like plucking off a false beard, and speaking in a normal voice would say:

"I fooled you, didn't I?"

But this did not happen. Instead of helping Arbelet by saying something, he left him to disentangle himself as best he could.

"At your age you ought—"

"I'm only fifty-three."

This was another way of embarrassing people, because he had the haggard look of a man over sixty-five.

"That may be, Uncle. But you've lived in the colonies. You've had fevers. . . ."

"And everthing else! I bet there are at least nine things wrong with me at this moment."

Could a simple, frank young man like Arbelet hold his own against him? In any event, what was Arbelet really doing there, in that dusty garage where poultry pecked, in the yard blazing with sunshine, and in that hotel tucked away at the edge of the national highway? For the children at Nevers, this was Grandmother's day. So it was for Arbelet, who was supposed to join his family at five o'clock at his mother-in-law's dwelling, bringing with him the traditional birthday cake.

Félix sensed this. He also knew that it would only agitate his niece's husband if he advised him to go away.

Thérèse entered the yard for a moment to throw something into the garbage can.

"I've written to a home run by monks."

Félix did not smile, nor was he astonished or indignant. No! He became crushing. No one could say why. He gained in stature, growing larger and more solid, to the point where a stranger might have wondered how the conventional Arbelet could have dared to talk to him about a home.

"It's not too expensive. All they ask is fifteen hundred francs a year, provided you do a little work."

Without turning a hair, Félix asked harshly:

"What work?"

Why on earth didn't the young man clear out? Didn't he understand? Didn't he realize that he was getting more and more involved in a world that was outside his scope?

"There are two sorts of pensioners," Arbelet explained naïvely. "Those who pay six thousand francs, and who, for the most part, are disabled and can't do anything. Then the others, who—"

"Who are the servants."

Arbelet gazed about him and had the audacity to stammer, "But here ..." meaning "Here you're not even that."

Félix, as though he had had all he could stand, turned and went to the end of the garage for the nozzle of the hose. While he was bending down he asked abruptly:

"Have you told the children that I'm their great-uncle?"

"No. I thought they were too young to understand."

"To understand what?"

He stood upright, defying Arbelet and the whole human race. Yes, to understand what? Whose business was it to understand? Who had the gall? Eh? For a moment it looked as though his big paw was about to tweek Arbelet's nose.

"To understand what?" he repeated.

"Your—your misfortunes ..."

"So I've had misfortunes, have I? Idiot, clear out!"

"We won't talk about it any more if you'd rather not. But think it over."

It was so pointless. So ridiculous, and so rash.

What followed was even worse! It was as though Arbelet, losing his head, was irresistibly impelled toward the unforgivable blunder.

"It doesn't matter to us, but after all, you might run into old friends."

Standing with the nozzle of the hose in his hand, the old man looked hard at him, as though turned to stone.

"Forgive me, Uncle, but it's for your own good. . . ."

"You were saying? . . . I might meet . . ."

He might have killed his niece's husband at that moment with a single blow from the brass nozzle of the hose. Just to try it. To make a change. To see what would happen. He had talked long enough about killing someone!

He was genuinely tempted. Caught in a sudden burst of sunlight, Arbelet, in his neat dark-blue suit and his straw hat, seemed exactly designed to play the role of victim. He even had the air of doing it on purpose! His Adam's apple leapt. He was evidently a little frightened, and forced himself to smile.

"Well, think about it."

And then there came a moment of enlightenment. It did not last long, scarcely long enough for Félix to close his eyes and then open them again. He had been wondering why he was so strangely affected by this conversation. Now he understood. It was Arbelet's resemblance to Penders! Not so much a physical resemblance, because at that time Penders had been only twenty-two and was wearing a uniform. But in some way a resemblance of category: the category of victim!

It was as though there are certain people who, like sheep, are destined for the butcher's shop. Penders had the same trembling of the lips, the same wish to look men honestly in the face, and the same vanity that caused him to seek to master his timidity.

"Well, think about it. I'll be in the café. My bus does not leave until five."

It was one of those days! A little earlier, when Arbelet had crossed through the kitchen, Monsieur Jean had noted his passing without really seeing him, as though he were a shadow deprived of substance. Now, as he departed, Félix kept his eyes turned toward him but no longer took account of his existence. He said, in the toneless voice he used when he was talking to himself:

"I'll really have to kill one. . . ."

Really! He had added that word to his usual sentence because he had not *really* killed that other man, Penders.

Besides, at that time, he had perhaps been even more of a sheep than Arbelet, with the long mustaches then fashionable, and if he had enlisted in an African regiment, it was because of the pictures in a volume of Jules Verne.

Penders and he . . .

To think that there had not been a single man, a real man, who understood, except perhaps their colonel!

What had they known at that age, Penders and he? It was all very well to put stripes on their arms and hang a revolver from their belts, to give them a few dozen wretched blacks to command. They still knew nothing, neither how one lives nor how one dies!

They still believed in make-believe, in pictures in books, which they sought to resemble. That was the truth. In the pictures, colonial soldiery plunged into the undergrowth to spy out the land. They had not done so altogether deliberately, but had been sent on patrol, as in the history books. And, also as in the history books, the blacks of their escort had melted away almost without their noticing.

The difference was that when they had found themselves alone, without provisions, which the blacks had stolen, they had been afraid of everything, of hunger, of the unknown, and even more of the night—with the fear of children, so intense that as darkness fell they had stayed huddled together. . . .

Meanwhile, there was Arbelet, who, not long before, adopting the manner of an adult citizen, had talked about arranging everything in the interests of all, everyone to have fifteen hundred francs a year, care for the aged and the infirm, religious institutions and God knew what besides!

That was how it had all begun, for Penders and countless other youths who had never heard his name. He came from the north, from the region of the Ardennes, and he thought he was strong because he had big knees, although, as Félix now knew, this was the result of malnutrition when he was young, from a diet consisting mostly of potatoes.

Thirst had driven him almost mad, and he had wept. Then he had turned in rage upon his companion, ordering him to go and find water. Félix had not known what to do. He, too, was thirsty and he had an overwhelming desire to stay alive.

When eventually he had got back to the army post, crawling literally on hands and knees, no one had believed that Penders had committed suicide without even warning him, all of a sudden, by thrusting the muzzle of his revolver into his mouth. Félix had been placed under arrest, as regulations prescribed. There had been talk of a court-martial. One day the colonel had come to see him, at once paternal and disgusted.

"Sign this, will you? It's your dismissal. You can go and get yourself hanged somewhere else."

And Félix had known that actually the colonel was right, and that he should not have allowed Penders to die. But how? That was another question. He should have thought of something. . . .

After that he had spent three months in a hospital, although without suffering from any particular ailment; simply because he could not adapt himself to the state of being no longer a child.

Then, without any period of transition, he had become used to being nothing at all! Used to living like that, without the need to be greeted by other men and not caring for their opinion. Used to living like a mushroom or a tree, eating and drinking, doing anything for anyone.

What did he care if he was no longer admitted to the circle that gathered to greet the arrival of a ship loaded with a fresh consignment of useful Penders? What did he care when he saw the veterans point him out, doubtless saying in an undertone:

"That's Drouin."

"What's he done?"

"A bad business, out in the rough country. He's finished! He shouldn't stay here. . . . It's irritating."

But not for Félix! He had come to take pleasure in irritating people and, to add to the embarrassment, he had gone to live with a black woman who was ugly. He joined with other natives in making the rounds in boats with junk for sale, and he had the impression that this was an act of revenge.

During the war he had been transferred to a noncombatant unit, and he had not cared.

For some years he had cleaned out the public conveniences attached to a railway station!

Then he had become croupier at a semiclandestine gambling club.

Then . . .

What did any of it matter? Should he have let himself sink still lower, perhaps become an ordinary bum? No. No one would have taken any notice of him, and he would not have spoken with anyone. No one would have given him orders, and thus he would not have been able to ruminate on the idea of killing someone.

He pointed the hose at the kennel to soak the bitch, for no reason, simply because the thought had occurred to him. It was he who had to drown her annual litter, as well as those of the cat.

What did it matter? Once, after he had put the newborn kittens in a sack, he had noticed crows in the meadow beside the Loire, and he had flung down the sack to see what would happen. . . . Had not the black woman with whom he had once lived killed one of her children at the moment of its birth because it was black and she was afraid of Drouin?

On top of all this, Arbelet, acting on the excuse that he was married to his niece, had come to his garage and dragged him out of bed, giving himself the airs of an honorable man—of a stupid obstinate sheep—and talked about homes and . . .

The dog was soaked enough and now lay miserable in its kennel with its tail between its legs. Félix pointed the hose at Thérèse's son, who had just entered the yard. He only wet him a little, and on one side, perhaps because the child was as lively as the devil.

"What are you doing here?"

"Go to hell!"

"Is it true that you've told your father everything?"

"It's none of your business."

Félix realized that the boy was almost one of his own kind.

"Have the police let him go?"

"I don't give a damn!"

And the urchin dodged around the old man, who was undoubtedly the only person in the world who impressed him. He was always looking for some trick to play on him, but never found one. Or, rather, his childish contrivances left Félix unmoved.

At a distance the two of them could be seen in the middle of the yard where the patch of sunlight was growing smaller. The old man, motionless on the paving stones, was casually directing the spray of water, which splashed on the ground a few yards away. The boy was keeping behind him, sucking a greenish lollipop. In its kennel, the dog was sadly licking itself.

Monsieur Jean was already putting the soup for the evening meal on the stove. Nine was washing dishes, still seated, because a bucket of hot water had been placed between her legs so that from morning till night she had no need to leave her corner.

Thérèse entered and said simply:

"He's back."

"Your husband?"

Mme Fernand, at her cash desk, was doing her accounts, and all the luncheon customers had departed.

In the café, a few minutes earlier, a clumsy and embarrassed Arbelet had attempted to delay Rose with light conversation.

"I bet all the customers chase after you, and that one or two have tried to take you away?"

He was no good at this sort of thing. He hoped for nothing. The entrance of the Pole, drunker than ever, had surprised him; but he had been even more astonished by the way the girl confronted him.

"No, I won't serve you anything. You're drunk enough already! Aren't you ashamed?"

"Go and get him."

"Who?"

"Your boss."

She'd already gained the assurance of manner Arbelet had noted among all the people belonging to the White Horse Inn.

"You get out! Don't be a fool. You know perfectly well that the police are keeping an eye on you."

"So I'm to let him sleep with my wife and I haven't even the right to have a drop to drink?" He was moving toward the counter, intending to serve himself.

Monsieur Jean entered, with a towel in his hand and his white hat on his head.

"Leave us, Rose."

He approached, not threateningly, as Arbelet would have expected, but with a placid fearlessness.

"You will be good enough to get out of here and keep you mouth shut."

Arbelet, who had risen, sat down again. He did not admit to himself that he did it in order to avoid becoming involved in the rumpus he foresaw.

"Get out! Go on, move yourself! My house is not—"

They came together, grappling. Perhaps a blow was struck by one or the other. Arbelet wondered if he should intervene, and again rose from his seat. It was at this precise moment that he received a blow on the head, from a siphon bottle flung by the Pole.

He did not at first realize that he had been wounded, and that it hurt. He stood with his hands on his forehead, but then he automatically looked at one of them and saw that it was covered with blood.

5

He now knew why, when disaster occurred, the haggard victims were like bloodstained ghosts. He caught sight of himself in a mirror, and it was not the pain, or the knowledge that he had been hurt, but his own reflection that stupefied him.

According to this reflection, he must have one eye sticking out of his head. There was no other way of accounting for it. There was no sign of the wound or the torn flesh, only blood running from his hair down to the corner of his mouth and, amid this flow of blood, the whiteness of an eyeball.

Arbelet did not cry out. He was standing, as though in a nightmare, with an air of pleading:

"Is no one going to pay any attention to me?"

He dared not touch his eye or even open his eyes enough to discover if he could see out of both. He heard Rose running toward the kitchen calling:

"Thérèse! Thérèse!"

Monsieur Jean pulled open a drawer, while the Pole got a switchblade knife out of his pocket and, without saying a word, pulled back the catch.

"You're going to drop that right away," said the proprietor, taking a revolver out of the drawer.

Mme Fernand, who had not left her post, was telephoning in an almost calm voice.

"Yes . . . You'll come at once, won't you? And let the doctor know on the way."

Everything seemed to happen in slow motion until Thérèse appeared and, brisk and decided, walked straight up to her husband, unconcerned with whatever risks she might be running.

"So you've gone mad, have you?"

She said it quite simply, as though she were talking to a naughty child, and pointed to the knife.

"Give that to me!"

Then, when she had it in her hand, she used the other hand to slap the man's face, and concluded:

"Now you can wait for the police."

That was the end of it. Now Arbelet could be attended to. Not by Thérèse, who was not interested, but by the proprietor and Rose, who moved toward him. At that precise moment, moreover, Arbelet felt his senses leaving him. He had just time to stagger back onto his seat, attempting to smile to excuse himself.

Félix, having finished hosing the yard, was sweeping the dirt into the gutter with a stable broom. He had heard the sound of the siphon falling on the tiles after hitting Arbelet, but had done no more than glance in the direction of the house.

Then Rose had appeared, calling for Thérèse, and Thérèse had crossed the yard.

Without hurrying, still with his broom in his hand, Félix had gone to the kitchen door and looked inquiringly at Nine.

"Her husband again, drunk as usual," said Nine.

Almost immediately afterward Thérèse had returned and, with a firm, decisive expression, had made for the staircase leading to her own room. Once inside she had gone to the window and cried out in the shrill, dragging voice used by women of the people in summoning their young:

"Henri! Henri!"

Henri did not reply. There was no way of knowing where he had got to. He might be quite near, within earshot, deliberately hiding himself from her, as he often did.

Félix wanted to know what Thérèse was doing up there, so he went to his own nook over the garage and hoisted himself onto the packing cases. He watched the maidservant pull her tight-fitting dress over her head. She seemed to be tidying herself. When he again had a glimpse of her face, she had a look of fury and was talking to herself, something like:

"So much the worse for them!"

A straw suitcase lay open on the bed. The wardrobe was also open. Thérèse, after coming and going, was leaning out of the window again, calling more loudly than ever:

"Henri! Henri!"

Being at the window probably reminded her of Félix's observation post. She could not see if he was there, but, just in case, she stuck out her tongue in his direction. It did not prevent her, still in a great hurry, from changing her underclothes; and the garments she had been wearing were in such poor condition that she thrust them under the wardrobe. She put on her better dress, and rolled up the other to fit into the suitcase.

Then, for no reason, she disappeared. She could not have gone downstairs, because Félix would have seen her through the window on the landing. Nor had she gone to the toilet, because the staff was not allowed to use those on the second floor.

She returned about three minutes later, went on with her packing, then shut the suitcase and went downstairs.

Out in the yard she stood looking about her and again shouting for Henri.

No one belonging to the household was in the kitchen except Nine, immobile in her corner, which that evening was bathed in a violet light. She watched everyone come and go. Rose filled a jug with hot water from the faucet near the stove. Then she heard the footsteps of several people on the stairs and soon afterward the same footsteps above her head, in one of the bedrooms.

The police had arrived and handcuffed the Pole, who was gazing slyly at the floor.

When Monsieur Jean had to pass near his wife, he gave her a brief, furtive glance, wondering how she was going to react; and it did not reassure him to see that she retained the placid expression of everyday.

"Take some clean towels to the doctor, Rose. Not thick ones, but the ones from the lower shelf."

One of the policemen went off with the prisoner, while the sergeant, a bony, fair-haired man from the north, seated himself in the café, crossed his leather-clad legs, and began carefully to fill a pipe.

"What will you have?" asked Monsieur Jean.

"Nothing . . . Well, a small marc. What did he want this time?"

"I don't know. He was drunk. I tried to turn him out."

The sergeant was content. He smiled at his glass of liqueur and at the café in general, bathed in cool dusk relieved only by a ray of sun, coming from no one could say where, which flickered on the patterned wallpaper.

Monsieur Jean, although he was not in the habit of doing so, poured himself a glass, which he swallowed at a single gulp, while the other man found it prudent to have a glance into the next room, where Mme Fernand was seated. Having done so, he got down to business.

"Did he say anything?"

Somewhat embarrassed, Monsieur Jean replied awkwardly:

"I wasn't listening."

"He's not a bad fellow. It seems that he'll behave perfectly well at the quarry for ten days on end, and then the need for drink comes over him and he disappears."

Monsieur Jean was wondering what Thérèse was doing. He supposed that she was upstairs helping the doctor.

"Who is the man who got hit?"

"I don't know. It's the second time he's been here."

"Will he bring a charge?"

Both men had a second glass, to while away the time.

Félix had gone back into the kitchen, not from curiosity, but simply to eat. Only Nine was there, and, without saying anything, he went to the refrigerator. He might have said:

"Thérèse is clearing out."

Because he knew. If he said nothing, it was not for the sake of discretion, but because he liked to keep everything to himself. He ate standing, taking a piece of meat out of the stew pot. He heard the sound of footsteps overhead, and since this was not usual at that time, he looked questioningly at Nine.

"A customer who got hit with a bottle," the old woman explained.

"What customer?"

"I don't know. The customer who was alone in the café."

If he did not laugh, it was because he never laughed, and perhaps because he was incapable of laughing. But he could not prevent himself from blurting out:

"I'm sure it's my niece's husband."

It was so unexpected that even Nine, who was never astonished about anything, found it a little strange....

"Have you got our bill, Mme Fernand?"

Everyone was more or less where one would expect: the proprietor and the sergeant in the café, and Mme Fernand at her cash desk in the dining room, talking to the young married couple, who had just returned from their daily visit to the Loire and in three days had developed a tan.

"Are you leaving this evening?"

"Yes. I have to go back to work tomorrow. We're catching the seven-fifteen."

"So you won't be dining here?"

"No. Perhaps you wouldn't mind letting us have something cold to eat on the train."

Félix and Nine listened without interest. All the doors were always more or less open. They saw Thérèse return from somewhere outside, having, evidently, left by the road at the back. They did not ask her anything or even notice that she was wearing her better dress. It is true that it was black like the other.

"You're to finish setting the tables, Thérèse."

Thérèse never answered "Yes, madame." It was a principle of hers. She never answered at all, but did what she was required to do with an air of pronounced sulkiness.

The fact is that everyone was waiting for something, but no one knew exactly what. Probably for the doctor to come downstairs with news of the injured man. The circle of light had vanished from the wall of the café and there was a heaviness in the air, a lowering sky, which seemed to threaten rain.

"Thérèse!" called Mme Fernand, still busy with the young couple's bill. "What did you serve number 3 this morning?"

"Same as usual, grapefruit juice."

"No coffee?"

"No. Why? Are they leaving?"

Félix, having finished his meal, was about to return to the yard. What delayed him was the sound of footsteps on the stairs, and of whispering. He saw the young man go up to the cash desk.

"May I have a word with you, Mme Fernand?"

She wondered why he spoke so solemnly, but Thérèse seemed to know. She left the dining room ostentatiously and returned to the kitchen, where she stood close to the open door.

Félix was too far away to hear. The young man talked in a low voice, and the proprietress only interjected a few monosyllables. At the end, however, she was heard to say:

"Come this way. As it happens, the police sergeant is here in the hotel."

Félix looked at Thérèse. The latter shrugged her shoulders with a bad-tempered expression and then, on a sudden impulse, ran upstairs to her room.

Nine watched her with mild surprise.

"Now what's the matter, Félix?"

"Nothing."

In the café it was Mme Fernand who was doing the talking, while her husband's eyes sank deeper into their sockets.

"I'm certain it's that girl," she concluded. "It's not the first thing that has disappeared. This time it's a watch belonging to a customer."

"What was the watch like, monsieur?"

"It was a gold wrist watch. I left it, as I often do, on the bedside table."

The sergeant turned to Mme Fernand.

"Where is Thérèse?"

"I think she's in the kitchen."

"Would you mind getting her?"

It came as a surprise, sometime later, to see a customer enter who appeared to be soaked through, since no one had noticed that a light but steady summer shower was falling. Mme Fernand was busy at the telephone.

"Hello! Is this the Garissol Grocery? Forgive me for troubling you, madame. I've an urgent message for your neighbor, Madame Arbelet, who does not have a telephone. Yes, Arbelet. Would you mind getting her?"

She had time to make a sign to Rose to attend to the rain-soaked customer.

"Hello! . . . Don't cut me off. . . . Is this Madame Arbelet? I'm calling for your husband, to tell you that he won't be coming home this evening. He's still in Pouilly . . . yes, at the White Horse Inn. Oh, no . . . It's just that some business has delayed him. Good night, madame."

As always happened on such an occasion, there were three times as many customers as usual, cars constantly arriving for no reason, and Thérèse not there to help with the service. The sergeant had borne her off in spite of the insults she showered upon him. Upon her return, she had stood in the doorway and summed up her hatred, not for the proprietor, but for Mme Fernand:

"Bitch!"

They had seen nothing of her son, who had been loitering somewhere in the streets. He had not appeared in the yard until a little before dark, and Félix had said to him casually:

"The proprietor is looking for you."

"Why have they taken my mother to jail?"

"I know nothing about it. Go and see the proprietor."

There were fifteen or sixteen diners at the same time. It was embarrassing to telephone the police in their hearing. Mme Fernand had dragged the boy into the kitchen.

"Go to you mother as quickly as you can. You know where she is? She has something to tell you."

At the police station an officer, with a gleam of mockery in his eye, was seated with his legs crossed, smoking a pipe.

"You might as well admit that you were trying to run! The proof is that your suitcase was packed."

"I'd had enough of that dump."

"Where were you going?"

"That's my business."

"You were waiting for the six o'clock bus, weren't you? And that's why you were looking for your boy."

He had repeated the question "Where is the watch?" at least twenty times.

She had not given way. Finally she had growled:

"It's the proprietress who invented the story, because she's jealous."

"Of you?"

"Do you think her husband wasn't always clutching at my skirt?"

"So you've already told me. That's enough of that. It's a queer taste that wants to make love with a slut like you."

He was deliberately provoking her, and was successful to the extent that Thérèse began to give details, using the coarsest, filthiest language she could think of.

"So now you know. Anyway, the boy once saw it all, and he can tell you."

Arbelet did not sleep, though he was not in pain. In order not to tire him, they had not left him a night light, but the rays of the streetlight gave vague shape to the furniture of the room.

There was nothing wrong with his eyes! They had not been touched! Nothing had been damaged except the skin under his hair, and what had so frightened Arbelet was like the effect of make-up—the flowing blood, encircling one eye, had given it a terrifying aspect.

Strictly speaking, he could have gone home. But they had urged him to stay, and he had allowed himself to be persuaded. He lay listening to the noises and wondering if Rose would come upstairs, as she had done once already, to ask if he needed anything.

There were people down below. The clatter of dishes, the comings and goings. Then, one by one, the cars departed.

By ten o'clock the sergeant and Monsieur Jean were alone in the café and the ritual of small glasses of marc had been resumed.

"I couldn't get anything out of the boy. As one would expect, she kept on denying everything. I couldn't find the watch in her suitcase or on her, although I had her completely undressed."

Why was there a gleam in his eyes? Particularly when he went on to say:

"As for the rest, she made no bones about telling us that she often took men up to her room. When this happened, she sent the boy to sit on the stairs. All kinds came to her, young and old, bums she picked up in the small bistro near the bridge."

Monsieur Jean did not trouble to look toward the next room, where his wife, who was finishing the day's accounts, could hear everything.

"I rather think," the sergeant went on, "that for a long time she's been wanting to leave for Marseilles, where she has an old boyfriend. You probably remember him. A very dark-skinned fellow, whom I arrested at last year's festival because he was threatening everyone."

For Arbelet, on the floor above, all this was nothing but an endless monotonous murmur. Nine had gone to bed, and the worst part of the day was over for her, the thirty-seven stairs she had to climb to get to her den.

Outside, under the striped awning, the two bulbs lighted nothing but the dripping of rain. The passing cars no longer stopped, except for one belonging to a nervous little man who had lost his way and gone past Sancerre.

Rose was having supper in the kitchen, and Félix, seated on a chair, was waiting to take up his post of night porter on the sofa in the passageway.

The minutes dragged by for Arbelet in a vast emptiness marked only by a click, which halved the light entering his room. They had turned out the lights on the terrace. A door closed. Footsteps sounded as the sergeant departed.

No one came to ask how he was feeling, and this depressed him. He failed to hear Rose's footsteps, but a streak of light appeared under the door leading to the next room, and at the same time he heard the voice of Monsieur Jean.

"Well?"

Then the voice of the proprietress:

"Well what?"

There were further sounds as the couple got undressed. Mme Fernand's voice was calm and continued to be, but that of Monsieur Jean, although he kept it low, was aggressive in tone.

"Is that all you have to say?" he asked.

She replied, no doubt seated on the edge of the bed, taking off her stockings, "What do you want me to say?"

"Nothing!"

There was a pause while they brushed their teeth. Then one of them got into bed.

"So you've decided to say nothing?"

The man had returned to the attack. It was evidently he who had been the second to brush his teeth, because he could be heard moving about. There was no sound from his wife.

"Listen! This isn't a good moment for annoying me. You know perfectly well what I am talking about."

"Come to bed."

"So after everything that has happened, you still have nothing to say to me?"

"What would be the use?"

"And you don't care, do you?"

"I'd just as soon not stir things up."

"But you knew? That's what you mean, isn't it?"

"Do please get into bed, and let's get some sleep. Anyway, the man next door with the injured head may hear us."

"As if I cared! For hours you haven't given me a single look."

"But I have! For instance, now!"

"And what does that look mean?"

"Nothing, Jean. I promise you. Don't make me say things that I don't want to say. We must hope that everything will settle down, mustn't we? That girl will go."

"Of course."

"Well?"

Arbelet was dumbfounded, almost alarmed. He had never imagined that things like this could happen between husband and wife. What was most extraordinary was that it was the husband who was in a fury.

"Well? Well? Is that all you can say? You keep everything to yourself, don't you? So you don't give a damn if I've been sleeping with Thérèse?"

"Jean!"

"What about Jean? And I'll bet that isn't all you've found out. But you never give a sign! You sit calmly at your cash desk. You know perfectly well that nothing enrages me more than that."

"Jean, get into bed."

"Into your bed, you mean, next to you, while ... Christ! ... I don't know what I'm saying. ... Never mind! It's you who asked for it. You disgust me!"

"If you shout like that, the whole house will hear you."

"I warn you that if you continue to play this game, I will do something desperate."

"How do you want me to behave? Do you want me to nag you? You can't help yourself, can you? You've always been like that...."

She had been born in the White Horse Inn, and for twenty-five years she had seen her father drunk every evening, to the point where, when he seated himself at the table of one of the customers, the whole household trembled. From seven o'clock onward anxious looks were exchanged. Her mother called to her in a whisper:

"Keep close to him."

They used tricks to keep the damage under control, but even when he was dead drunk, he was more cunning than any of them and knew exactly what they were up to.

Then, as Jean had just done, he flew into a rage. His rages were terrible, because he broke things for the sake of breaking them, and sometimes he struck blows.

Jean did not drink, and he took touching precautions in his pursuit of the maidservants. Afterward he would glance anxiously at his wife.

"I simply think that you should be more careful," she said. "Rose's father came back here. At noon he was drinking with Stephan at the Café du Pont."

Jean no longer knew what line to take. He would have liked to go on being angry.

"What does that matter to me?"

"You know what sailors are like. One evening when he's drunk . . . And his daughter's still a minor."

Arbelet could not see the action, but he seemed to see it after it had happened. The proprietor, in his exasperation, had seized the first object that came to hand, a pot or a vase, and flung it on the floor.

"Calm yourself," his wife said.

He laughed jeeringly.

"Easy enough to say! Calm yourself! Calm yourself! You're calm enough, you are! You've always been calm. From the moment you had your hand on the cashbox and the money came in."

"Would you rather that I burst into tears and scolded you? . . . Where are you going?"

Evidently he was moving toward the door.

"I don't know."

"Jean!"

"Hell!"

He opened the door, and she jumped out of bed and ran barefoot after him.

"Stay here! Do you hear me? You've got to stay. We're going to have enough trouble as it is."

She shut the door. He stayed. She got back into bed, and he quickly followed her. The light went out.

It seemed to Arbelet that a small feminine voice inquired in the darkness:

"Are you crying?"

That was all that happened that day.

6

Christian noticed nothing, but Emile was so struck by the event that years later he remembered the history lesson on Charlemagne they had that day, and which he repeated fluently from memory, spitting out the words like marbles while his mother set the table.

The window was open on the quiet street. Months of rain had not washed out the figures Emile had drawn in chalk on the bricks of the opposite wall.

The house consisted of four rooms, as in a child's building game, two on the ground floor and two upstairs. The dining room, in front, served also as the sitting room, and behind it was the kitchen, where they ate their morning meal, "so as not to spread the dirt."

Next door was the grocer's shop and Mme Garissol, who also sold vegetables, kerosene, and tickets for the national lottery. Now and then one heard the ringing of the bell.

"Someone wants to speak to you on the telephone, Madame Arbelet."

And Mama had gone out just as she was, in her apron and with her hair in curlers. When she came back, Emile was struck by a change in her, which he did not quite understand. She did not seem unhappy or angry or agitated. She smiled as she said:

"We may as well have supper. Your father won't be coming back this evening."

Nevertheless, she made one think of a character in an American film who has just had a knock on the head.

There was a kind of amazement on her face. While she was eating, she kept her eyes fixed on the dusky evening street, and forgot to see that the children were properly served.

Upstairs, the door between the parents' bedroom, which was in front, and that of the children was always left open. Long afterward, as he was falling asleep, Emile heard the sound of his mother's hairpins falling into a glass bowl as she withdrew them from her hair.

Next morning, when he kissed his mother before leaving for school, he knew from the smell of the house that it was washday. One couldn't be sure whether it was going to rain or whether the weather would be fine. The sky was blue, but there were gray clouds fringed with ominous white.

Emile had not washed properly, for no particular reason, but probably because things were not quite in order. As he walked to school, he rattled his ruler against the house fronts.

While he was on his way, Mama said to Marthe, who came three times a week for the washing and housecleaning:

"Will you look after Christian for a moment, Marthe?"

She hurried around to Mme Garissol, whom she did not like, in order to telephone. At that hour of the morning, Mme Fernand was not at her regular post in the White Horse Inn. There was no one near the telephone. Monsieur Jean had gone out. He could not be far away, because he had not put on his cap, but he was not there. Perhaps he was at the police station.

Rose had just gone upstairs with a tray. Félix was sweating in his attic. So the telephone continued to ring in emptiness until poor Nine, after clapping her hands over her ears, decided to get up and move slowly toward it. She was not used to the telephone.

"Yes, this is the White Horse. . . . No, it's not the proprietress; it's Nine. . . . What did you say? . . . I didn't catch what you said. Who is speaking?"

Nine was suffering. Besides, it hurt her legs to have to stand up.

"What gentleman? . . . A gentleman from Nevers? . . . I don't know. . . . There is one, the one who was hurt, but he hasn't got up yet."

Hearing this, Germaine Arbelet was almost relieved.

"How much do I owe you, Madame Garissol?"

Maurice had been hurt! At least that explained why for the first time in all the years of their marriage he had not come home at night! It also explained the unhappy effect that the phone call of the previous evening had produced on Mme Arbelet. She had been greatly perturbed, for no serious reason, and if anyone had asked her what was wrong, she would have replied:

"I don't know. But something's going to happen."

So that was it! Maurice had been hurt. She returned home, and after that her actions were decided.

"We won't bother with the linen today, Marthe. Or, rather, do only the colored ones. I've got to go out. I don't know whether I will be back in time for lunch. Look after Christian."

She went up to her bedroom and dressed herself as carefully as though it were Pentecost. Christian, absorbed in his own affairs, did not see her leave, and only asked for his mother about noon, when he saw that the table was not being set.

Don't panic! . . . That would do no good. . . . Germaine started thinking in the bus, and when the ticket collector

69

approached her, it occurred to her to ask him a question.

"Have you already done this trip today?"

"Only the first part. As far as Sancerre."

"You don't know if there's been an accident somewhere near Pouilly?"

"I haven't seen anything. Wait. I'll ask the driver."

No; the driver had seen nothing either. They ran through a heavy shower and then emerged into sunshine. If it was not a road accident, then what sort of accident was it? Was it possible that her husband had quarreled with Uncle Félix, and that he was responsible?

What struck Germaine when the White Horse Inn came in sight was that there were four or five people standing about not far from the door. She told herself that it was not today that her husband had been hurt, and so the onlookers must be there for some other reason.

She got off the bus and walked past. The hotel terrace, after the rain, was drying in patches. She entered by the restaurant, saw no one, turned toward the café, and was struck dumb with surprise.

There were two policemen in there! One of them, a big blond, was seated at a table writing. The other was standing close to Thérèse, who was crying and talking at the same time, sometimes muttering in a low voice, and sometimes shouting as loudly as she could.

The proprietor was also there, dressed in white, with his hands in his pockets, watching the scene.

"Excuse me, monsieur. . . ."

"One minute, if you don't mind."

Thérèse, without taking any notice of her, went on:

"When I tell you that it was the boy, you've got to believe me. He's always prowling all over the place. He saw the watch on the bedside table and took it without thinking, just to play with it. The proof is that I found it in the pocket of his overalls, and it was broken."

"Your son says that's not true," said the sergeant severely.

"And I swear to you that he is lying."

"I'm more inclined to believe the boy. I questioned him for two hours and he didn't contradict himself once. While as for you, well, we all know what you are...."

"Please, monsieur," said Mme Arbelet, again trying to attract attention to herself.

Without even looking at her, Monsieur Jean signaled to her to keep quiet.

"I'll tell you exactly what happened," the sergeant impatiently began. "You've been planning for a long time to go after your boyfriend in Marseilles. You were talking about it three nights ago in the Café du Pont, which is where you go to pick up your companions for a night or for an hour. Who went with you down to the riverbank on that particular evening? Because you don't even need a bed!"

"That's my business. Here, I've been made to do it standing up in the cellar!" Her tears had dried.

"So you decided to leave, and when you found that there was trouble with your husband, you went and packed your bag. You had to wait for the six o'clock bus. You thought of the watch, which you'd seen on the night table, and you did not know that the people were leaving that same day and were bound to notice the theft when they came to get their things together."

Thérèse glared at him with hatred, and he looked pleased with himself.

"Do you dare to say that that is not how it happened?"

"You've got it all wrong!"

And now she turned her glare on the proprietor.

"This one is going to be made to pay for it. When I see Rose's father, I'll tell him everything. All the disgusting things they do together at six o'clock in the morning, and the tricks he's taught her. He hasn't even got normal tastes!"

"Please excuse me!" cried Germaine Arbelet in desperation, as greatly dismayed as if the sergeant had suddenly stripped himself naked in front of her.

"What is it?" he asked.

"I've come to find my husband."

"Are you Madame Arbelet?"

The proprietor hurried toward her.

"Come with me. It was Nine who spoke to you on the telephone, and I am afraid she upset you for nothing. . . . This way . . . Look out for the step."

That morning Christian had taken no notice of his mother's departure, although she had gone to kiss him when she was dressed for the street and had her hat on. As for Germaine, she now was scarcely aware that she followed the cook dressed in white up a staircase, then along a tiled corridor. What was occupying her thoughts was the story of a watch.

What watch? She knew nothing about it. A nightmare watch, a furious girl who cried and threatened, a self-pleased policeman . . .

"He's perfectly all right. It was nothing but a stupid accident, which—" Monsieur Jean tapped on a door and was called upon to enter. Germaine found her husband in bed with a bandage on his forehead and, standing by the doorway, a very pretty little maidservant holding a tray.

"Come in, Germaine." He smiled, the somewhat pallid smile of the sick or the injured; but she had already felt something like a twinge of mistrust.

72

"Is there anything that you want?" asked the proprietor before withdrawing. He went out gloomily, making Rose go in front of him, because he had no wish to look at her.

Germaine, still on her feet, asked:

"What happened to you?"

"I was in the café waiting to see your uncle ... "

As the words passed his lips he realized that they were false. It was a half-lie, uttered not for the sake of lying, but to keep the story short; not to have to explain that he had already seen Uncle Félix and that he had decided to speak to him again before leaving, and that meanwhile he had sat waiting in the café, having nowhere else to go. All this would have taken too long.

"I was in the café waiting to see your uncle. A man came in, a drunken Pole, who began to shout. The proprietor tried to make him leave, and he threw a siphon bottle at him. I was the one who got hit."

There was nothing extraordinary in this. Why, then, did Maurice Arbelet have a sense of embarrassment as he told the story, as though he were hiding some shameful secret?

His wife sensed this awkwardness, which is why her manner scarcely softened, only enough for her to ask:

"Is it a deep wound?"

"No. It only broke the skin. I was expecting to leave here in about an hour, after the doctor changed the dressing."

"Did it hurt much?"

"I didn't feel a thing at the time, only afterward. . . . But wait. I'm going to get up."

At this moment a brief sentence was uttered, barbed as an arrow:

"So in fact you haven't seen Uncle Félix?"

"Yes, but—"

"I mean you haven't been able to talk to him."

"Yes, I have. Let me explain. . . ."

But it was too late, and he knew it from Germaine's expression. And, knowing it, he talked like someone who is lying and who, moreover, knows that he is suspected of lying.

"I'd seen him already. But he was so unfriendly that I decided to . . ."

This was not what was worrying Germaine. She was, instead, recalling the impression she had got the previous evening, when she had talked on the telephone at Mme Garissol's. There was danger in the air; she did not know what. Her husband, unsuspecting, had got up and was dressing.

"Why didn't *you* telephone?"

"Yesterday? I couldn't have gone downstairs. I had a slight temperature."

"But this morning?"

Yes, why hadn't he done it? The truth was so stupid when it was confessed. Although he was in the habit of getting up at seven, he had not awakened until about half past eight, and then, such was his feeling of comfort in the warm softness of the bed and his half-dream, he had no inclination to move.

"Nobody called me," he said awkwardly, and sought to change the subject by adding, with an aggrieved expression, "You haven't even kissed me!"

She did so obediently.

"You see, the people here were so upset about what had happened that they didn't know what to do with me. If I'd left right away, they might have thought . . ."

"What might they have thought?"

Exactly! It was a stupid story. In the next room, Mme Fernand, having completed her toilet, opened her door and paused for a moment in the hallway listening to the

74

voices. When she went downstairs, she glanced into the café, where the sergeant was questioning Rose.

"You say you've never seen this watch? Would you regard Thérèse as an honest person?"

"I don't know."

"Would you have trusted her with money?"

"I don't know."

Thérèse had her eyes fixed hard upon her, while Monsieur Jean, behind his counter, was affecting an air of glum indifference. When he saw his wife enter the next room, he went to join her.

"They've found the watch," he said gloomily.

"Where?"

"Among the boy's belongings. Thérèse says he's the one who took it."

He was overwhelmed with troubles. A single glance had been enough to assure him that his wife's attitude had not changed since the previous evening. She was behaving like someone who has seen and heard nothing, or someone to whom all things are equal. She patted her hair in front of the mirror.

"Have you got the menu?"

"I haven't done it yet." He bent over the desk, picked up a pencil, and, forgetting that it was indelible, moistened it between his lips.

"I've got some shrimps left. I'll order a rabbit pie."

He had no heart for the work.

Mme Fernand pointed to the ceiling.

"Is that his wife who has just arrived?"

"Yes."

"What did she say?"

"Nothing. I don't know. And anyway, hell, I've got enough trouble already!"

It had all come so suddenly, when he least expected it.

He'd had enough, that was all! He went into the kitchen, where there was no one but Nine, in her corner by the window. He would have liked to burst into tears. He did not; he flew into a rage instead, paced the room, and went out into the yard, where for two pins he would have kicked the dog.

He repeated, without wanting to, "I've had enough! I've had enough!"

At that moment no one could have persuaded him that he was not a victim. Whose victim? And of what? It was hard to say, but, for one thing, there was his wife, who had said almost nothing since the previous evening, as though she did not wish to soil herself with all that filth.

But what had he done? He'd slept with two of the maidservants. So what?

"Jean!"

He did not look around. His wife must be standing in the doorway. There was a white hen near the tip of his shoe.

"The doctor's come."

"All right. Let him go up."

He greeted him, nevertheless, almost affably, because that was business. He sent Rose for hot water and shrugged his shoulders when he found that there was no longer any need for the bandage around Arbelet's head and that a small strip of adhesive tape would do. Arbelet seemed ill at ease.

"Jean!"

Good! He had been called to from below. The sergeant wanted to leave.

"That's it! I've finished here."

"What have you decided?"

"I'll send in my report. She'll be charged with theft and receiving. Meanwhile, I'll take her with me, and keep her while we wait for the magistrates to make up their minds."

A shower had just ended, and the sun shone brightly on Thérèse, who was getting ready to leave.

"Are you going to put handcuffs on me?" she asked mockingly.

"No need. You won't get away. Get moving!"

She was about to go through the doorway when Mme Fernand appeared.

"What are you going to do about the boy?" she asked the sergeant.

"I don't know yet. I suppose he'll go to the child welfare authorities."

She made no comment; neither did Thérèse. It was better to get the business over. The departing group crossed the terrace, past its green-painted furniture.

"Why did you ask him that?" asked Jean, without looking at his wife.

"No particular reason."

She went back to the cash desk, saying, "If you'll give me the menu, I can get started."

She opened the till and got out some accounts while he wrote the words *lobster mayonnaise* and then crossed them out when he remembered that they didn't have enough lobsters available. Finally he decided to go and have a look in the refrigerator.

On the way downstairs, Arbelet, holding his straw hat in his hand, ventured to ask:

"Shall we try again to talk to your uncle?"

"No. Anyway, it was your idea. I knew perfectly well that it would be no use."

They entered the sunlit dining room, and Mme Fernand came smilingly to meet them.

"Surely you're not leaving like this! It's nearly noon. I very much want you to have lunch with us. What can I bring you in the way of an apéritif?"

"Nothing, thank you. We're leaving at once," said Germaine firmly.

"There's a bus at half past one that takes you straight there."

"The children will be waiting for us."

It was not true. Marthe was there to see that they were fed. The tables in the dining room were covered with shining white cloths, and on the sideboard were baskets of delicious-looking fruit.

"My husband will make you a very special lunch."

"I assure you, madame . . ."

Germaine was inclined to be shy, always rather more polite than was necessary. Nevertheless, Mme Fernand did not persist. She, too, was a woman. And Germaine's words had been enough for her. They had been accompanied by a smile. A smile of gratitude? And also by a glance at her husband and then at the door.

"*Au revoir,* madame."

"I am so sorry."

A little farther down the street, they passed the bakery where, on the Monday of Pentecost, they had bought the croissants. They went on and stood at the bus stop. From there they could see the whole length of the road that runs through Pouilly, between two rows of restaurants and shops, and then, mounting a fairly steep incline, vanishes into the country.

"You aren't feeling bad?" asked Germaine.

"No . . ." But then Arbelet corrected himself. "Well, only a little."

"Don't stand in the sun."

The sign of the White Horse Inn hung suspended

against the blue of the sky. Arbelet, for no precise reason, was feeling a heaviness of heart, and also, among other, confused, sentiments, threads of greater trouble, bitterness, something like rancor, and even a slight impulse to rebel. He was recalling the huge form of Uncle Félix in the hotel yard, and feeling the weight of the gaze that looked him up and down, a gaze heavy with contempt.

For now he was sure that it was contempt!

"I didn't think of asking for my bill," he suddenly remarked.

It had not been intentional, and he gave no thought to running back to the White Horse to rectify the omission.

"That does it!" retorted his wife. "What time do you have?"

Emile returned from school and was dismayed to find the house empty of his mother, with Marthe, who had put on a clean apron, doing the cooking. It was queer! As queer as the night before had been without his father.

And, despite the sunshine that filled the yard, where Marthe had hung up the colored linen to dry, it was a little disquieting.

Talk was scarcely possible on the bus, because of the noise. All the heads were nodding to the same rhythm, all eyes intent upon the road. Arbelet could not put on his hat because of the wound. Germaine sat holding her bag with both hands on her knees.

7

Thanks to a salesman who was not feeling sleepy, they had had to stay open until eleven, and Monsieur Jean, who was suffering from indigestion, had found himself obliged to play backgammon with him, game after game.

Finally, he had gone upstairs. The door of his room, number 7, could be heard to open and close as he put his shoes out in the hallway. A single bulb was burning downstairs, and Monsieur Jean, at the counter, was surveying the rows of bottles and considering what he would have to drink. Half in and half out of the doorway, Félix stood waiting, with his ragged blanket draped over his shoulders.

The proprietor, conscious of his presence behind him, behaved as though there were no one there and poured himself a glassful of a rather strong liqueur.

"Why are you looking at me like that?" he finally asked.

And Félix replied, with his eyes fixed upon him:

"I'm not looking at you."

It was almost true. He was not looking at Monsieur Jean; if he saw him at all, it was only because he happened to come within his field of vision. But the way he spoke the words made them sound like either sheer silliness or deliberate insolence.

Monsieur Jean gave him a nasty look, very brief but very black, as he was in the habit of doing when his thoughts were hard and ugly.

"Have you been drinking?"

Without waiting for a reply, he went on, leaving the bar and turning out the light in the café, "If you can't decide to keep yourself clean, one of these days I'll throw you out."

He knew that the old man was waiting to lie down on the faded sofa, which, during the day, customers made casual use of. He glanced with disgust at the sagging seat, shrugged his shoulders, and, in a bad temper, with a burning in his stomach, went up to bed.

Félix watched him every step of the way, then tossed his blanket onto the sofa, scratched his head behind his ears, and undid the greasy collar of his shirt.

That idiot up there had asked him if he had been drinking! And he did it the way a person does who knows what he's saying and who doesn't stand for that sort of thing!

"Just the same I'll have to . . ."

To kill someone, of course! But it probably would not be Monsieur Jean. It would be . . .

He lay down and stretched himself out with a sigh. Reaching for the switch, he plunged himself into the obscurity in which nothing is to be heard but the creakings of life in the house, scarcely as loud as the sound of mice in the walls.

"I'll have to . . ."

He felt that it was going to begin, that this was one of those nights. . . . He did not fight against it. He could not have said whether he was glad or frightened. Voluptuously, he slid into it, while his breathing became more irregular and his face grew damp with sweat.

Monsieur Jean had talked about alcohol because it was the obvious thing. The fact is that Félix had drunk so much in his time, as much as an entire bottle of Picon before his noon meal, that now he could not smell a glass of anything without feeling sick. For at least ten years drink had meant nothing to him, and it was only rarely that he accepted a glass of wine, just to try it again.

Besides, he had no need of alcohol. This thing came over him by itself, as now, after a certain kind of day. There were no absolute rules, and he himself was sometimes mistaken. Other people more often suspected other causes. The proprietor, as he had that evening, thought he was drunk. Old Nine looked at him as she might have looked at a sick child and said, nodding:

"You're having another attack of fever."

On these occasions he had an alarming way of looking at people. For example, he would stop abruptly in front of them and stare at them with fixed eyes. Or else he would follow their movements and gestures as though he had never before seen a living person.

He rapidly grew hot, then suddenly shivered. Yet he was almost certain that it was not the outside temperature that was responsible. Or the stormy weather, or any nonsense of that kind.

Shock was at the bottom of it. Never mind what kind—a word heard in passing, a news item in the paper, an unexpected sight—anything at all might produce this state of excitement. Holidays, such as July 14 or Christmas, had the same effect. But this time the reasons for excitement were numerous—the arrival of his niece's husband and the things he had said, then the business of the watch, the police, and Thérèse, who had showered them with coarse abuse.

"Just the same I'll have to . . ."

For an instant he held his breath, because he had heard something, a faint noise on the staircase. He silently switched on the light and raised his eyebrows as he saw that it was Rose, coming downstairs with her shoes in her hand.

"What are you doing?" he asked her in a low voice.

"I've got to go out for a minute."

"What for?"

Without worrying about him, she was putting on her shoes.

"Answer me! You're going to meet Thérèse?"

Because, if Thérèse had been found guilty of theft, she must have been let off with a conditional sentence. She had arrived during the evening, taking advantage of the fact that it was the dinner hour and that there were customers present.

Defying everyone, she had marched through the restaurant and gone up to her room, where she had collected her belongings. Rose, in the kitchen, had announced:

"She's here."

Monsieur Jean had gone on with his cooking, and Mme Fernand had kept her eyes on the customers.

"You're going to meet her, aren't you?" Félix repeated.

"It's no business of yours."

"Provided I don't say anything to the boss."

"If you do, I'll tell him that you're a dirty old man and that you spy on us in the morning."

She opened the door and vanished into the darkness outside. For a moment Félix forgot to turn off the light. Then his hand reached for the switch. His thoughts were following Rose, who could only be going to the Café du Pont, because no place else would be open at that hour.

"I'll have to . . ."

This brought him to the boil much more quickly than he had expected. As a rule, it took a certain amount of time to decide on his prospective victim. He had already killed Monsieur Jean at least ten times in his imagination, and he was no longer interested in him. Mme Fernand was more tempting, because she was neat and quiet, and he was moved by the thought of the look on her face when she found herself stark naked in front of a threatening Félix.

Before Rose came down he had been on the point of deciding on his niece's husband, who would certainly return one day or another. But now the catch had been released. It had to be Rose! The temptation was all the greater because at any minute she might reappear in flesh and blood!

Félix was sweating again and breathing with difficulty. He could not have said whether he had his eyes open or shut. But he saw the least detail. The first thing to do was to get the towel hanging behind the bar counter.

He'd stand behind the door and wait. It would not be for long. Thérèse would have sent for Rose to tell her something, or to make plans in case of further police action. The Café du Pont closed its doors at half past eleven at the latest. Rose would hurry back, because she would be scared, and she would scratch on the door, to avoid ringing and arousing the proprietor and his wife.

And then . . .

He lived it all intensely, going through every movement in his mind and in its proper sequence.

He saw Rose, gagged with the soiled towel from the bar, stretched on the sofa in his place. Standing over her, he took his time, because he could do whatever suited him.

And this was where it would be necessary to choose, to decide what would be best, so as to have no regrets afterward. It must be the maximum or it would not be worth doing at all.

Perhaps . . .

He was not like other people, like the customers, like all the men who made advances to Rose, seeing in her nothing but a pretty girl of sixteen, a fresh and juicy morsel. He had spied on her at moments when no one else was looking. Moreover, he had his own way of looking at people, of seeing them in advance, so to speak, and knowing what way they would go in the future.

For example, he could see Rose when she had reached more or less the condition of Thérèse, as would surely happen. And it was almost certain that she would become as savage as the other woman. You could detect it in her voice when she threatened, "If you do, I'll tell him . . ."

Her voice and everything else! She was by no means an innocent little girl, but a wench who had got off to a bad start.

Thérèse had told her that Félix watched her every morning through his spy hole, and she had been ashamed. Yet she had submitted at once to Monsieur Jean's requirements, doing so in the same way that she served the tables.

Félix went back to the beginning, where he was standing by the door, because his mind had become confused. His thoughts had taken a new direction, and he no longer saw Rose in his place on the sofa.

Well, she scratched on the door and, with the towel in his hand, he . . .

But why at the same time did he see Arbelet standing with a look of astonishment in the passageway and asking for a bedroom? He drove his niece's husband away, and then encountered the contorted face of Monsieur Jean, with that black look that characterized his bad days.

"I'll have to . . ."

He turned over heavily in his dampness, but opened his eyes when he discovered once again that Arbelet resembled Penders. Perhaps they didn't have a single feature in common, but that made no difference, because Félix sensed that they were exactly the same kind of men. So much so that when he recalled Penders huddled at the foot of his tree with is mouth open, it was his niece's husband whom he saw, looking at him in supplication. As for Monsieur Jean, he . . .

He heard the sounds of hurried footsteps on the road, but ignored them. Rose had to scratch for some moments on the door before he rose heavily, hesitating to switch on the light, and grumbling:

"Just the same I'll have to . . ."

The thought made him feel ill. He had a pain, he did not know where; but he grimaced like someone who is suffering. He pulled back the chain, turned the key, and saw the door handle turn as it was operated from outside.

He stayed rigidly motionless by the door as it opened and Rose entered, bringing with her the freshness of the night. She paused in astonishment, seeing no one in front of her, and then discovered Félix.

"What's wrong with you?"

His hands were deep in his pockets, the fingernails pressing into his palms. All he found to say was:

"You've been out to get yourself ——?" The sentence ended with a crude precise word. She laughed mockingly.

"Why not?"

She moved backward to the foot of the staircase, then ran upstairs, while Félix, thinking of nothing, replaced the chain and turned the key.

"I'll have to . . ."

His eyes were watering, and there was a tingling at the tips of his fingers. While he was pulling the cover over himself and switching off the light, he sniffed and moaned:

"Will I ever be able to . . ."

It was unfair! He couldn't do it! He couldn't do anything! He was as confused and bewildered as a great sick animal bumping aginst the bars of its cage.

Surely it would have been natural for just one person, just once, to show a little understanding?

He was not dead, like Penders, true enough! Was it his fault? He had been only a youth, like his companion. Neither of them had known anything. They had seen life in terms of picture books.

If Penders had fired a bullet into his mouth, no doubt it was because he had been hungrier or thirstier. And Félix had been so dull-witted that he had stupidly watched him do it, without understanding.

He had not admitted this at the inquiry. He had declared:

"My back was turned at the time." It was not true, as he knew very well! The other man had warned him, and had even added, "If you get back to France and you run into my sister . . ."

Was not Penders the guilty one? Guilty of everything. Because, after that, all normal life had ended for Félix.

When he drank, he was regarded with disgust.

When he lived with the black woman, because no white woman would have anything to do with him, people looked as though it were enough to make them sick.

And the worst thing of all was that when he was a croupier in Paris, he had been dismissed because of his bad breath!

Was it just? Was it fair that no casual acquaintance or passer-by had ever . . .

"Just the same I'll have to . . ."

Poor idiot that he was, was he going to spend his life repeating those words without ever having the guts to strangle a little brat of a girl as he might twist the neck of a hen?

He had fever, all right. A new attack had come. He

would not be able to wash the car of the salesman who played backgammon. He would be shouted at. . . . And tomorrow he would have to remain stretched out on his mattress, sweating and shivering, with a constant throbbing in his head. Who would bring him anything to eat? Thérèse was no longer here. Rose would be afraid of him, perhaps. And if the weather was fine, they would have all they could do to serve the customers, the men and women passing by in their cars. . . .

At this moment Monsieur Jean was lying beside his wife in the big walnut bed. If he had the least temperature, or if he simply began to breathe a little too heavily, Mme Fernand would wake up and gently turn him over onto his other side.

Did she weep in the mornings, when she pretended to be asleep, while he went to visit the maidservants? And was it because she wept and the traces had to be removed that she took so long over her toilet, so that when she came downstairs it was always with the same artificially pink countenance?

Félix was not sleeping. He never slept. He simply thought in a different way with his eyes closed, seeing jerky, incoherent images. But never for a moment did he lose the sensation of being there, bloated, heavy, and dirty, lying on the pink sofa or on his mattress over the garage. Sometimes he grunted like an animal, opened his eyes, and stared fixedly at some point in space, without losing anything of his sense of torpor.

He could have taken a dose of quinine, as other ex-colonials did, but that would have brought down the fever, and fever was almost his only possession.

When it reached its climax, he could feel every drop of sweat making the effort to dilate a pore, to take shape, and to hesitate on his skin before melting into the others. He was convinced that he was conscious of the working of his internal organs, and of the missed beats of an old heart that had never been in good order.

But none of this altered the fact that, after living so long like a stray dog, eating any garbage offered, sleeping anywhere and anytime, and catching all the diseases, he was still twice as strong, at the age of fifty-three, as a man like Arbelet, who was only thirty-five!

Putrescent, certainly, but strong: there were trees like that, which cling to life longer than the others.

A door opened and closed; that was the toilet on the next floor. Perhaps it was the salesman. Or perhaps Monsieur Jean had a stomach ache.

Suppose he were to creep silently upstairs and wait for him to come out into the darkness of the hallway . . .

"I'll have to . . ."

His most harrowing recollection was the way Penders had done it. When it happened, it had seemed as natural as calling someone on the telephone.

For a long time, they had not spoken. They no longer had the strength to go on walking, and both were wondering if anyone would think of sending out a party to look for them. Penders had been seated with his back to the tree. Suddenly he had sighed and said:

"I can't stand it any longer! I'm getting out."

It was then that he had added, in a friendly voice:

"If you get back to France and you run into my sister . . ."

Félix no longer remembered what he had asked him to do—something quite ordinary, like giving his watch to a friend.

Penders had taken his revolver out of its holster. It was

one with a circular magazine. He had removed all the bullets, then had put them back and had tested the muzzle between his lips.

Félix could not have guessed that it would happen so quickly. Penders had taken the muzzle out of his mouth, stared at it, making a face, perhaps because of the taste, then, a second later, he had pulled the trigger.

That was all!

Félix staggered up, for after those nights he was always unsteady on his thick legs. Letting his cover fall to the floor, he went and released the chain, turned the key, and opened the door to let in the sunshine. To complete the job he should have carried the garbage cans outside, but he did not feel strong enough.

He did not know whether he was hungry or whether it was some other discomfort at work in his chest and stomach.

There was movement above his head. He entered the kitchen, and was surprised to find himself confronted by old Nine.

"What are you doing here?" he asked.

"Nothing."

She was only a few minutes early, but the fact struck him as extraordinary.

He was not well. He needed to calm himself. The dog was tugging at its chain.

"I'm going to lie down."

"Fever?"

He did not reply. After crossing the garage, he stopped twice in climbing his ladder, with the sudden feeling that he was a very sick man and that perhaps this time would finish him off. The thought alarmed him, and, from bravado, he climbed onto his two packing cases to see Rose, to find out if the proprietor had come to visit her, to . . . His features hardened as he looked through his spy hole.

Rose had covered her windows, on one side with a towel and on the other side with an old skirt, which prevented him from seeing into her room.

"I'll have to . . ."

He had been robbed even of this! He had been a fool, the night before, not to . . .

He sat down on the edge of his mattress, forgetting to stretch out. Penders had also been seated when . . .

He had to cry out, and he did so, but it was an appeal to Nine.

"Nine! Nine!"

The dog made it a pretext for barking, drowning his voice. He had to wait.

"Nine! Nine! Somebody!"

He was trembling. He was afraid. He heard sounds down below, near the cars.

"Up here! I'm ill. Will someone come up?"

It seemed to him that his sweat was growing colder, and it occurred to him that he might grow colder still this way.

Nine could not climb the ladder.

"I'll go and tell Monsieur Jean," she cried from down below.

And suppose he stopped breathing!

He was so frightened that he did not dare lie down, putting himself already in the posture of the dead.

He sat waiting with a hand pressed to his thumping heart, and listening to a cock crowing in the garage, to which another cock, two houses away, replied.

8

"What's the matter with him?" asked Mélanie, piling up plates with a clatter, and Nine, bloated and pale, bathed in her morning sunshine, replied, with a wag of her head:

"It's his fever."

It was as though for her fever had a sort of individual quality. When she dragged herself out of the kitchen, her slippers slithering over the tiles, it was due to "her" legs. Where other people were concerned, it was "their" eyes or "their" stomachs.

But it was not worth explaining this to Mélanie, who was no longer thinking about Félix. If she had asked the question, it was because, looking through the window, she had seen Dr. Chevrel's small gray car in the yard, standing midway between sun and shade.

Mélanie was almost a member of the household. She lived with her four children two streets away, and it was she who was called upon when extra help was needed. On holidays she came of her own accord. She knew where everything went and she did not talk like a stranger.

"If I were Monsieur Jean, I'd have done something about it, but I wouldn't have turned her out. She's going all around town telling stories. If the boy's father hears even half . . ."

The morning was particularly bright, and one might have thought at times, in places where the air lay stagnant under the sun, that there was a flavor of honey. In the kitchen there were at least ten wasps buzzing around Mélanie. And Mélanie was working like a horse in harness, without pause and without thought, going straight ahead, and making a great deal of noise.

Surprisingly, Mme Fernand came downstairs before her usual time, fresh and neat as a new pin, with the shadow of a smile that she always wore. What was even more exceptional, she went first into the kitchen.

"Good morning, Nine. Good morning, Mélanie. Is the doctor still here?"

Then she went into the dining room.

The butcher's truck had just pulled up at the door. It was going to be a hot day. The asphalt was already glistening, as it sweated between the stones, and the street smelled of tar. In the garage, hens were pecking the ground, and two of them were chasing one another, each telling the other what she thought.

Monsieur Jean had been the first to climb down the ladder. The doctor followed, trying not to get too dirty. At the bottom he brushed his trousers with his hand, wiped his fingers on his handkerchief, and exclaimed in astonishment:

"How on earth can he live in all that filth?"

The proprietor replied:

"If I gave him a proper room, in two days it would be in exactly the same state. He does it on purpose."

They walked the few steps to the door of the garage and stood there side by side, gazing into the sun-filled yard, where the dog, at the end of its chain, lay watching them with a hopeful air, perhaps waiting for a friendly word.

Monsieur Jean asked in an irritated fashion:

"Well, what do you think?"

The doctor was young but already accustomed to seeing people die, generally by their own fault.

"It's a severe attack of malaria."

"You think it may kill him?"

"He'll survive this time, but of course one can't tell. . . . "

At the top of the ladder, Félix, his skin glistening and his eyes hazy, had succeeded in getting off his mattress and scrambling to the edge of the gallery to hear what they were saying. The two men, standing at the edge of the sunshine, looked like figures in a shadow play. The proprietor had his hands in the pockets of his white trousers; the doctor was lighting a cigarette, the smoke of which cast on the ground a shadowed pattern finer that a spider's web.

"What can be done?" asked the proprietor, troubled in spite of himself.

"Quinine," answered the doctor, who could not care less. But then, after a pause, he said, hesitantly:

"You'd do better to send him to the hospital. The man's rotten through and through. One of these days something more serious will happen to him, and then perhaps it won't be possible to move him."

Félix, crouched on all fours in order to hear better, caused a board to creak. The two men heard the sound, but paid no attention to it.

"In your position, with a hotel like this, you don't want to have a seriously sick person on your hands."

Félix was holding his breath, so as not to be heard down below.

The doctor moved toward his car, but then added:

"If the quinine doesn't work, call me. I'll give him an injection."

"Has he got syphilis?"

"I don't think so, although I haven't examined him from that point of view. But acute cases of malaria are treated in the same way. . . ."

Another surprising thing was that Mme Fernand had ordered the meat without talking with her husband. She had even been in the café, since Rose was busy upstairs, to serve a passing customer who wanted a glass of beer.

The doctor was opening the door of his car. Monsieur Jean suddenly made up his mind.

"I wanted to ask you something about myself," he stammered, glancing sidelong at him. "Could you possibly come upstairs for a minute?"

Félix did not go back to bed, although there was nothing more to be heard. He was swaying, but he gazed in terror at his mattress, feeling that if he gave way, they might come and take him when he was too weak to resist, and move him to the hospital.

He contented himself with sitting on the edge, holding his head in his hands, his elbows on his knees. Before long, he began to sway sideways, from left to right. And he had the feeling that the world was rolling, which recalled an experience at sea, he did not remember where: a flat, sickening sea, stirred by an invisible swell. He listened to the wings of flies and the cackling of the hens. He heard the sound of traffic on the road, voices more or less distant; all this was distinct but in another world.

He thought, mustering all his energy, "I must get up." But he gave himself a few more minutes, to recover his failing strength.

"I must get up. Otherwise those bastards will come . . ."

He was cold. He had nothing left to drink. With eyes closed behind his two hands, he did not know what he was seeing—landscapes that perhaps were not real, or were formed from moving fragments of reality that overlaid and melted into each other; lights and colors, and acute pain in his left side, and always that sense of swaying, which suddenly caused him to vomit the water he had drunk that morning.

The act of vomiting made his eyes water, but he was not crying. He stood, clinging to one of the packing cases, which he had used in the morning to spy on Rose. He must wait for this to pass. Above all, he must not lie down; he must not give way!

The sound of wooden shoes came from the yard, followed by the cool sound of water being splashed around from a bucket. The wooden shoes told him that this was Mélanie, who had evidently been called in to fill the gap while they were looking for someone to replace Thérèse.

He stood swaying like a bear. When the doctor had come to see him, he had greeted him with the words, "Well, you old pachyderm."

Suddenly he began to wonder which was the more prudent course. If he got up and went down to the yard, would they not take advantage of the fact to make him get in a car and be taken to the hospital? On the other hand, if he lay clinging to his mattress and obstinately refused to move, would they resort to force?

And suppose he had a loaded revolver? What about that? What would they be able to do? He knew exactly where to find a revolver—in the third drawer of the cash desk.

He was almost tempted to laugh. All he had to do was to wait for the right moment, and then make his move. And after that . . .

He was so relieved, and the sense of swaying had become so pronounced, that he nearly fell asleep.

On a day like this there might easily be thirty parties for lunch, and there was still nothing on the stove. Mélanie came only to finish the washing-up from the night before and to do a bit of dusting in the kitchen, which was never very clean. When she heard the proprietor go up to his bedroom with the doctor—the same one who had attended her at her last two childbirths—she asked Nine:

"What's the matter with him? Is he sick, too?"

Cars were passing, endless cars, and their glittering bodies gave such an impression of luxury and gaiety that they made everyone want to go out.

Seated at her desk with her accounts, Mme Fernand saw them, but her expression changed only when one of them stopped.

"Mélanie!" she ordered from the doorway of the kitchen. "Go and tell Rose to come down even if she hasn't finished the bedrooms. It's time to set the tables. And as for you, go and get cleaned up."

Two or three times she looked up at the ceiling and was astonished when the doctor left with only a casual good-by, instead of coming to shake her hand.

A little shiver ran down her back, and she had to make an effort to go on with her work, but she scarcely raised her head when her husband passed in front of her on his way to the kitchen.

As a rule, when he suffered from indigestion after a meal, his face had a leaden color, his eyes narrowed, and his general expression became quarrelsome. But from the glimpse she had had of him, his face looked altogether more alarming. His teeth were clenched as though he was afraid he might bite someone. He was as white as a candle, and his eyes were so glazed that he might be expected to stumble from not being able to see ahead of him.

"Jean."

She said this in a voice that was at once humble and firm. He hesitated, and was on the verge of not stopping.

"Shut the door."

She meant the door of the kitchen, because all other doors were always open. Wasn't that how they always lived, with open doors and people more or less everywhere?

She remained seated; he stood facing her and waited.

"What did he tell you?"

She would rather have kept silent, and not to have had to wait for his reply. Her flesh was creeping with fear. It was terrifying to question that white face and those eyes, the eyes, above all, which seemed to see nothing but chaotic images. He replied, nevertheless:

"What are you talking about?"

He was trying to be evasive but was too distressed to succeed. He was wearing his blue-checked trousers and his white blouse with two rows of buttons and clasps at the elbows. Only his chef's cap remained of his working clothes.

His wife was looking at him as she never had before, with a mingled expression of supplication and fear. She murmured:

"Was the answer yes?"

"What are you talking about?"

"You know very well."

He trembled visibly and bowed his head. She went on:

"Thérèse was sick, wasn't she?"

He was incapable of answering and preferred to plunge into the kitchen, open the stove, and vigorously poke the fire, so that flames rose from the smoldering embers. By this light he appeared less pale. Suddenly he turned and looked toward the window, where Nine was seated. It had seemed to him that she, too, was staring at him in a pointed manner.

"What's the matter today?"

"Nothing, Monsieur Jean."

He had to go through the everyday routine to have something to hang on to, otherwise he felt he could scream with rage, fear, and despair. He opened the refrigerator. Then he put his head into the dining room.

"Did you order mutton?"

"Yes."

"We served it the day before yesterday." The telephone rang. His wife answered.

"Very well, Monsieur Chapuis . . . Certainly. I understand. . . . For eight? . . . Have a good trip, Monsieur Chapuis."

He looked in again.

"It was Monsieur Chapuis, telephoning from Fontainebleau. They're arriving quite soon, in two cars. Eight places. He wants *quenelles* and a *croûte aux rognons.*"

Rose came downstairs, having combed her hair and wiped her face with a damp towel. Mme Fernand said gently to her:

"A table for eight for Monsieur Chapuis, near the window. Haven't they brought any flowers this morning? You'd better go and get some at Billon's."

"Very well, madame."

For the sake of something to do, Mme Fernand filled a carafe with water and went out and watered the laurels. She made the journey three times, and the third time she thought she caught sight of the figure of Thérèse, and the uniform of a policeman close beside her.

It was the end of the waiting period. Two men and a woman got out of a car, in a hurry to move on, because they wanted to reach Nice the same day. They ordered sandwiches.

Rose got busy. Mélanie, who was several inches taller

than anyone else in the house, was clumsily setting the tables. She had changed her wooden shoes for black felt slippers, because she said she could not walk in shoes.

Dr. Chevrel was visiting an old man on the point of death somewhere on a farm on the other side of the Loire.

Monsieur Jean, the tightness in his throat remaining, went through the dining room into the café, and was startled to come face to face with Félix. At first he was speechless. The figure of the night porter, who still had his blanket around his shoulders, was truly like that of a ghost. One had to either laugh at his unearthly aspect or else be afraid.

"What do you want?"

"Nothing."

"Well, what are you doing in here? Why aren't you lying down?"

By way of reply Félix merely laughed, and while the proprietor poured himself a drink, a pale-green apéritif, he retreated backward and staggered out to the yard. Instead of crossing it, and returning at once to his retreat, he installed himself outside the kitchen window.

The big flabby face of Nine was visible behind the glass. There was a grin on Félix's face as he drew a large regulation revolver halfway out of his pocket, the same kind of weapon as Penders had used.

The next minute he went on his way. He was pleased. He had frightened Nine, who watched him vanish into the darkness of the garage.

"Are you there, Jean?"

"Yes."

From her place in the dining room, Mme Fernand could not see behind the counter in the café, and on that particular morning everybody was wondering where everyone else was.

"What are you doing?"

"I'm drinking a glass of wine."

It was not true. He was drinking almost neat Pernod, though with a sense of revulsion, knowing that in a little while he would feel a burning in his stomach. He saw Thérèse, who was going along the sidewalk on the opposite side of the road, the shady side, deliberately stop at a doorway to chat with the butcher who dealt in horseflesh.

"I think there's something burning," said Mme Fernand.

"I'm coming."

Was it by instinct that the explanation of Félix's presence had suddenly occurred to him? In any event, he automatically pulled open the third drawer and noted that the revolver was no longer there. He was about to pass in front of the cash desk when a voice stopped him, as it had done before.

"Jean."

"What?"

"Listen. I know what you're worrying about. You ought to know that it's not so very serious. It can be cured."

Chevrel must have been talking to her, to her and not to him! She should have prepared him, and approached the matter more tactfully. As it was, he answered, with a sardonic laugh, "You don't say?"

She wanted to add something, but glanced toward the end of the room, waiting until the person concerned could not hear. She had to be quick about it. There were people everywhere, and, moreover, new customers would be arriving.

"About her . . . It would be better if you said nothing."

He understood. He knew from his wife's glance that she was referring to Rose.

"I'll speak to her myself."

He had to prepare *quenelles* for eight and a *croûte aux rognons.*

What got on his nerves most was the fact that nothing escaped him. He could guess at people's expression with his back turned. Even the placid countenance of Nine was not like that of other days!

"What's the matter with you? Will you answer me?"

"Nothing, Monsieur Jean."

He ran a hand over his face, in a nervous gesture he was to repeat often that day.

"Why are you looking at me like that?"

"I am not looking at you, I swear."

Well, suppose he just carried on as usual? For a whole hour, bent over his table or the stove, he thought about nothing else but his work.

"Business as usual!"

The thought had become fixed in his mind, like that phrase in the mind of Félix:

"Just the same I'll have to . . ."

Business as usual! His wife. The White Horse Inn. And everything else. What would other people say, the ones who arrived by car and who were always in a hurry to eat, if they found themselves anchored as he was at the edge of a national highway?

"More flowers on the table for eight, Rose. It's for Monsieur Chapuis."

She went to arrange them and found herself close to Rose, who was folding napkins in a fan pattern and putting them in the glasses. But with Rose Mme Fernand could afford to take her time. It was not a matter of an hour or a day.

"You'd better throw a few buckets of water over the terrace. Or . . . no! Mélanie can do it."

Rose gazed at her in astonishment. There was a quite unaccustomed gentleness in Mme Fernand's voice.

As for Félix, no one knew what he was doing. It is true that everyone at that time was busy with his own work, coming and going with dishes and glasses and plates. The tables were beginning to fill up, resounding with innocent holiday gaiety.

To start with, Félix had got some big blue enamel jugs out of a cupboard, those that were used in the rooms in the annex, where there was no running water, and which were called one-night rooms. He had filled three to the brim and slowly, with pauses, he had carried them up to his own place. He was swaying so much that one might have thought he was drunk. Once, he suddenly stayed motionless for a good ten minutes, without even taking the trouble to put down the jug, as though he had been struck with paralysis.

It was Nine who saw him most often, because she was in the right place. The sun, now fully up, did not fall upon his hair or his body, but only on his feet, wrapped in shapeless rags. At one point he was noticed by Monsieur Jean in front of the open refrigerator, but the proprietor supposed that, as usual, he was there looking for scraps to eat. When he crossed the yard for the last time, he scarcely knew where he was, such was his state of confusion. He looked at the dog and the dog looked at him. Félix thought:

"Perhaps this is the last time."

The last time for what?

He remembered how once when he had been instruct-
ed to clean out the kennel he had found, under the straw,
a quantity of gnawed bones and stale crusts of bread: the
private store, in short, that the animal had collected. Up in
his attic, the night porter arranged around his mattress, or,
rather, between the mattress and the makeshift partition,
everything he had laid his hands on: the three jugs, a
whole sausage, a ham bone on which there was still
enough meat for three days, a loaf of bread and some bis-
cuits.

For a long time he stroked the revolver, until he was on
the point of trying it, merely to make sure.

"Just the same I'll ..."

But then he changed his mind, and his leitmotif, and
said:

"And now ..."

He didn't have the energy to take his quinine right
then. He collapsed on his mattress, with one arm out-
stretched, his mouth open, and his breath hot.

A quarter of an hour later, one could not have said
whether he was asleep or in the process of dying. As with
some dogs, his eyes were not tightly closed, but allowed a
streak of white to be seen.

9

Mme Brochard had been saying:

"I can't help wondering if it doesn't run in the family."

They were discussing her brother, Félix. She was far from having exhausted that grave subject, but her eye was suddenly caught by a border of Japanese carnations and she asked:

"Where did you get the seed? At Berthelot's?"

"No. We always go to Van Damme's."

Mme Brochard could not long sustain the tension of a serious or painful conversation. Her instinct recoiled from it, causing her to discover, enlarged as though by a magnifying glass, some object that attracted her gaze and, for the moment, became of primary importance.

It was a sort of recreation. She smiled instinctively at the sun and the heat that caused the air around the brightly colored carnations to quiver like water on the verge of boiling. Specks passed in front of one's eyes without one's knowing what they were or why the vibrations stirred the blue of the sky.

Just as in fine weather one could see the bottom of the sea, so here one had the impression of hearing, at a great distance, things that were not noticeable on other days—the opening and closing of doors on distant streets, a baby crowing beyond the barracks, the electric saw of the carpenter who had repaired the Arbelets' table, and the sharp ringing of the recess bell in a boys' school.

The sounds succeeded one another, merged and mingled, and then separated. Of this confusion Mme Arbelet retained only a single, dominating note, isolated in a moment of calm, of which she knew the meaning. In the same way, the garden for her was as fixed and definitive as a photograph.

The two women were seated at the back of the house, where the brickwork was less ornate than in front. There was light-colored gravel on the ground, a small table, two ordinary chairs, and two deck chairs, and, in addition, a large red balloon, which belonged to Christian.

Beyond this, separating the cultivated part, was a border of big stones brought home from their Sunday outings. There were carnations and, on the right, a plum tree. Roughcast walls enclosed this rectangle, three yards long and six wide. Beyond were similar rectangles belonging to other people, and other houses that had inferior brickwork at the back.

Germaine Arbelet was sewing. Christian, seated on the ground, was poring over a picture book spread open on a chair, which he was using as a lectern. He always found it necessary to change the purpose of things.

Mme Brochard was wearing her best dress, her cameo, and her ring with the ruby surrounded by small brilliants.

Interest in the carnations waned. The period of recreation was over.

"What were we talking about? Oh, yes . . ."

Her daughter was used to this.

"And you really think there's nothing to be done?"

"I am sure of it. I have never told you much about it, but your grandfather was a bit like that. He would suddenly go off on his own without saying a word to anyone. We would search for him everywhere. And then one day a letter would arrive from the other end of France telling Mother to come and join him with the children."

A brief pause. She didn't have the time to seize on a thought that passed through her mind.

"Since he was always talking about going to live in America, we always thought that was where he was. . . . When you think that I have a garden as big as this one and that I don't make any use of it!"

Germaine waited. It was best. Her mother would never cease to regret having rented the ground floor of her house, keeping only the upper floor for herself.

"When I tell you that they are the people who complained to me about Bobby because he once did his business in the hallway!"

At the sound of his name, Bobby raised his head. He was a small dog with a smooth red coat and a shortened tail. He waited for a moment, watching his mistress with his head on one side. Then, with a sigh, he lay down again in his patch of sun.

"So I said to them . . ."

Thus the hours slipped lazily away, amid the scent of flowers, the buzzing of flies, and whiffs of the rabbit that was stewing in the kitchen.

Germaine was surprised to see Emile appear with his satchel, announcing in a loud voice:

"I'm hungry!"

Why should the words have brought a question from Mme Brochard?

"Is your husband still satisfied with his standing in school?"

"Oh, yes. Maurice is satisfied with everything."

"It's true he has a nice nature."

Germaine was on the edge of mildly qualifying her mother's remark. But it was better not to speak of it, never to speak of it. Most troubles arise out of talk. To speak of them is to define thought, feelings, and desires that perhaps would never have become important in silence.

So Maurice had not changed. He always got up in a

good humor and went and woke the children by pulling
their noses. He sang as he performed his ablutions, with
unexpected interruptions when he was shaving.

"Love is the child . . ."

Two strokes of the razor at the corners of his mouth, a
grimace, and then, in a different voice:

" . . . the child of Bohemia . . ."

The windows would be open, and dew would be spark-
ling in the garden. Germaine would scatter crumbs for the
sparrows and watch them while she prepared breakfast.

No, Maurice had not changed. Anyone would have said
that he was just as cheerful as before, with a touch of in-
genuousness, which was at the root of his character.

It did not worry him in the least if people turned to
look when he brought Christian back from his music lesson on his shoulders and Christian ruffled his hair. "Here
I am, taking my family for a walk," his faint, quizzical
smile seemed to say.

When he got back from the office, he dropped into his
armchair, near the door to the kitchen.

"What are you thinking about?" Mme Brochard suddenly asked her daughter.

"Nothing."

It was so flimsy, like the faint look of nostalgia that
sometimes passed over Maurice's face.

"What's bothering you?" Germaine had once asked.

"Me?"

He was genuinely astonished. What could have been
bothering him?

Yes, what was happening? He was not in love with anyone; that was certain. Because he could not fall in love all
at once with a little servant girl who happened to be in his
bedroom when Germaine had rejoined him at the White
Horse Inn.

She knew this well. He was never in love. Only sometimes when they were out walking, he would look around mechanically at a woman—particularly at young girls. He knew this did not escape Germaine, and the first thing he did was to say:

"She had a funny sort of hat!"

At the same time he realized that she was not deceived, but, since it was not serious or worth the trouble of going into long explanations, he looked at her with smiling eyes, as though to say:

"You know, it's nothing really."

Lately, however, he did not look back at passing women; instead, he had sudden fits of melancholy. If his wife caught him in one of these dreaming moods, he was not frank with her. He hurriedly smiled or told some story, with forced good humor.

"Maurice!"

"What?"

"Tell me what's wrong with you?"

"But there's nothing wrong with me! What on earth should there be?"

It was wiser to say no more, not to get him to describe his unsettled spirit. All the more reason for saying nothing to Mme Brochard, who was suddenly struck by the smell of rabbit.

"Do you still do it in the same way as we do at home?"

The front door opened and closed. Germaine started.

"Emile! Hurry and set the table."

Maurice Arbelet entered the garden and bent over Mme Brochard's forehead.

"Good afternoon, Mama."

Germaine looked at him and saw that all was well—that is, his seeming good humor was sufficiently natural.

One had to go gently, that was all, not nag or do anything to ruffle his feelings. He kissed his wife and bent down to seize Christian and lift him high over his head into the sunshine.

"Well, you great bear?"

Held up at arm's length, the little boy, who was used to it, made no protest and continued to twist a length of string as peacefully as he had been doing when he was seated on the ground.

In the living-dining room Emile was spreading the tablecloth.

At the hottest part of the day, when Monsieur Jean had to mop his face every other minute with his towel and one could scarcely bear the heat several feet away from the stove, a party of customers arrived, the sort who drive a big convertible. Without bothering to consult the menu, they ordered a *châteaubriand à la Béarnaise.*

Monsieur Jean heard the order, because he always moved to the half-open door when new customers arrived. He came close to saying that it was impossible.

"It will take at least half an hour," he snapped at Mélanie, who passed the message on to the customers. She came back and announced, "That's all right. They'll go for a stroll while they're waiting."

He nearly ruined his Béarnaise, and only rescued it with a copious addition of flour. Sweat was pouring down his face. There was a pinched look about his nostrils, like that of someone on the verge of fainting. Since morning there had been a fixed look in his eyes, a look that was painful to endure. He had already repeated to Nine, who never opened her mouth, "When are you going to stop staring at me?"

He worked hastily and angrily, revenging himself upon his material.

He avoided looking Rose in the face, but whenever she passed near him he gave her an anxious sidelong glance, such as he directed at his wife when he was conscious of some wrongdoing.

Rose took no notice. She was behaving just as she usually did. She, too, was hot, and when she had made the journey between kitchen and dining room a number of times, there was dampness on the back of her neck and behind her ears.

"Two *soles meunières,* two!"

The dining room was crowded. Cars poured along the road as though it were the day of the Tour de France bicycle race. Chapuis, who had reserved eight places, turned out to have a party of twelve, having picked up some friends on the way. Since there were some pretty women among them, he acted the part of a regular habitué of the establishment.

"Where's Jean?" he asked Mme Fernand.

"At his stove."

"Can we go out there?"

He was one of those people of overflowing geniality who find it necessary to maintain a constant flow of laughter and pleasantry.

"Well, great chef! What about lunch? Come on in, everyone! Come and see Jean, the master chef, in the exercise of his functions."

Monsieur Jean contrived to receive them with a weak smile, which disclosed the points of his teeth.

"Can we take our places?"

"Certainly! You will be served at once."

There was no table large enough for twelve available. One of the marble tables from the café had to be brought in and the whole service changed.

Sometimes Mme Fernand looked toward the kitchen

door, and every unpleasant detail, added to those that had preceded, gradually transformed her feeling of impatience into anguish. Yet she could not leave her place. Noises and the sound of voices told her her husband's state of mind.

"Rose! They want something at number 5."

"They want the bill."

"What have they had?"

"The eighteen-franc lunch, a half-bottle of Pouilly, and coffee."

"No liqueurs?"

"No."

She had to direct the people who came to ask where the toilets were, although this was written up in large letters. Others inquired as to the price of rooms and full board, although they knew that they would not be coming back.

Mme Fernand smiled, a colder smile than that of Monsieur Jean, but less furious.

"Tell me, madame, which is the best road to Lyon?"

Rose and Mélanie dashed to and fro with trays and dishes, both being hailed by different tables at the same time. They called out their orders as they went down the step at the kitchen door.

"Two *poulets cocotte* . . . One rare steak."

Nine looked involuntarily at Monsieur Jean every time, and every time it added to his exasperation. This reached such a point that eventually he left the room and stood in the yard, panting and looking completely worn out.

Mélanie appeard in the kitchen.

"Three orders of chicken, three . . ." Then, not seeing the proprietor, she asked anxiously, "Where's he gone?"

Nine nodded toward the window, and Mélanie opened the door.

"Monsieur Jean! I need three orders of chicken."

If he went back, it would be a matter of chance. He felt quite capable of letting the whole thing go to the devil.

Never had he cut up a fowl more quickly. He literally flung the pieces on the plates.

"There you are!"

At first he had had something to think about, but he no longer had any need to think, nor was he capable of doing so. He was in a state of rage for the sake of rage! And, like a passenger in a car who instinctively makes a forward movement to help it up a particularly steep slope, Nine never took her eyes off the proprietor, to support him to the end.

In an hour at the most it would be all over. Things were already beginning to slow down. There were calls for the bill. Only the party of twelve over which Monsieur Chapuis presided was still at the fish course.

"Ask the proprietor to come here for a moment."

Rose obediently did so:

"Monsieur Chapuis is asking for you."

He had to change his expression, and wipe his forehead and hands.

"A round of applause for the chef who has prepared this marvelous dish for us. One—two—three!"

Monsieur Chapuis was beaming. He did his utmost to persuade Monsieur Jean to sit down with them, saying to his guests:

"To think that in all the five years I have been coming here he has never given me the recipe."

If he only knew, the well-meaning idiot!

"Forgive me, ladies and gentlemen, but I am wanted in the kitchen and . . ."

"You'll promise to come and join us for coffee?"

"I shall be delighted."

He was on the verge of tears when he re-entered his

kitchen, which was almost dark compared with the sun-filled dining room. He had avoided his wife, but it had seemed to him, nevertheless, that she had looked at him the same way Nine had, with the desire to encourage him.

Encourage him to do what? Could either of them have said? And the girl, Rose—why did she seem undisturbed? Or had they not yet told her what the trouble was?

He drank a glass of water, then a second and a third, and the icy liquid made him feel sick.

There were perhaps not more than another twenty minutes to be endured. The Chapuis party had reached the cheese stage. Mélanie, standing in a corner of the kitchen, was using her fingers to eat a slice of ham that had been left on a plate.

Rose happened to pass close by Monsieur Jean, and without thinking he gripped her by the shoulder.

"Has my wife spoken to you?"

She stared at him in consternation, alarmed by this sudden attack, and she did not answer immediately.

"My wife has spoken to you, hasn't she? She's told you everything? Answer me."

"Yes."

"Well?"

She did not understand what he wanted, but she felt him to be so threatening that she did her best to give him the sort of answer he was looking for. She glanced appealingly over his shoulder at Nine, who could do nothing.

"Say something, can't you? For God's sake, say something!"

He had raised his voice, a thing that never was done in the kitchen, because customers in the dining room could hear.

"You refuse to speak?"

"But, Monsieur Jean . . ."

Quite suddenly, and for no apparent reason, he had begun panting, his mouth half open.

"She's told you what's wrong with you? You know now, don't you?"

Rose made a face, which ended in a sob. And Mélanie, upset, turned her face to the wall to indicate that this had nothing to do with her. The door opened, and Mme Fernand came in.

"You're wanted at table 8, Rose."

Monsieur Jean was disconcerted by the blank his mounting anger had encountered. To fill it, he felt impelled to pick up a dish, a salad bowl, and fling it on the floor, shouting:

"Hell and damnation! I've had enough!"

"Jean!"

"What about Jean?"

She nodded toward the dining room, and he gave her his most ferocious scowl, having been reminded that he was not privileged to indulge his suffering at his own convenience.

"I said hell, do you understand? It's finished, over and done with! I've had enough."

Mélanie contrived to get out of the room without being noticed and shut the communicating door behind her.

"They'll soon be leaving," said Mme Fernand, in a last attempt, which meant, "Control yourself for a few more minutes. After that we can argue and quarrel and shout and dance with rage. . . ."

But he was dancing already, with the rage of an angry child. He knew that he had started badly, that he would meet nothing but emptiness, and this only heightened his fury.

"Enough! Yes, enough!" he finished in a lower voice. Flinging his apron into a corner, he went out into the yard.

There was no point in following him. Mme Fernand returned to her desk and forced herself to smile at Monsieur Chapuis, who had inevitably heard the noise.

"Mélanie . . ."

"Yes, madame?"

Perhaps he would leave, as he had done on some previous occasions when he had flown into a rage. Once, he had not returned until midnight, and rather than enter his bedroom had lain down on the nearest unoccupied bed.

He might be still hesitating in the yard, but Mme Fernand heard sounds coming from the café. She could not see anything from where she was seated, and she called to Rose.

"Is that Monsieur?"

"Yes."

"What's he doing?"

"He's drinking."

So much the better. Strong drink made him feel ill at once, and there was nothing he could do but lie down.

"Serve the fruit, Rose."

Mélanie, having gone through the kitchen, found no one in the yard, where the dog was whining because it was time for her noon meal and she had been forgotten. Nine, with a great effort, had risen from her chair to close the door of the stove, which Monsieur Jean had left open.

There was a sound of footsteps on the stairs. Mélanie, realizing what this meant, went to tell Mme Fernand.

"He's gone upstairs."

"You're sure?"

"Well, listen."

A moment later they heard the sound of a door being slammed and the creaking of a bed.

"You must excuse my husband, Monsieur Chapuis. He's not feeling very well. The heat . . ."

"Only on condition that you have a drink with us."

She did so, and at last they got back into their cars. Then, for no real reason, and certainly with no definite suspicion, she went into the café and pulled open the third drawer behind the counter.

The drawer was empty. The revolver was no longer there.

For a moment she stayed motionless, then she broke into a run, dashed up the stairs, and flung herself with clenched fists at the door of their bedroom.

"Jean! Jean! Open up! Answer me!"

He did not reply, but he moved.

"Open the door! I must speak to you."

He deliberately made no response, and for the first time, she lost her self-control. She rushed down the stairs. Rose was clearing the tables. Mme Fernand went into the kitchen, where Mélanie was talking to Nine.

"We've got to do something! I don't know what. Should we telephone the police? Monsieur has gone upstairs with his revolver."

Alone in the dining room, Rose turned her head, seeming to ponder, and, going to the kitchen door, said diffidently:

"You're sure he had his revolver?"

"Why do you ask?"

"Because . . . I am not quite sure . . . but it seems to me Félix took it."

Mme Fernand, wasting no time, dashed into the yard, which she crossed on unsteady legs.

10

For the first time in her life, she talked to herself, as women do who have suffered misfortunes. Stumbling as she went, staring behind her at the window of their bedroom, she babbled:

"He's so high-strung."

But that is not exactly what she meant. The expression, as she applied it to her husband, had for her a special meaning of its own. Certainly he was high-strung in the sense that he was always excited, but there was an element of slyness in his manner, a hint of malice, of which he was unaware—because he was a man and had been born like that.

She did not notice the chickens in the garage, which she usually never entered. She looked uncertainly about her and called:

"Félix!"

She saw the ladder, climbed two or three rungs, and was stopped by a voice shouting:

"What do you want with me? Go away!"

"It's I, Mme Fernand. I want to—"

"I'm telling you, go down. Go away!"

She was hardly surprised, having so much else on her mind. Mostly she was afraid that Jean might do something stupid while this was going on.

"Listen, Félix, I—"

"All right, then! I'm going to fire."

He could not be seen, only something black moving in

the darkness above. Mme Fernand ran out just when a shot was fired, but Félix must have fired into the air, because a slight sound came from the woodwork of the garage. She ran across the yard, murmuring, "He's mad!"

Crossing through the kitchen, its occupants rigid with astonishment, she cried:

"Félix is mad!"

Then the staircase and then the bedroom door.

"Jean! Félix has gone mad! He has shot at me! You must come."

The door opened. Her husband looked somberly at her and remarked, as though it were a reproach:

"You aren't wounded?"

"I swear he shot at me. . . . Where are you going?"

Of course he was going to the garage. He had never been afraid. Mme Fernand had to run after him and grip him by the shoulders.

"Wait, Jean! The police will be coming!" And she cried out to the others, Nine, Mélanie, and Rose, it did not matter who:

"Telephone the police. They must come immediately."

Her bosom was heaving tumultuously. Never before had she been in such a state. Even the fringe of hair above her forehead was in disorder.

"Wait, Jean. Keep cool. I shouldn't have got so upset."

She tried to smile to give him confidence. She knew all about him and knew that sooner or later this would end in a burst of tears.

"Stay here. The police will do whatever's necessary. It's their job."

He let himself be held back, staring at the ground while he waited.

"It was bound to happen sooner or later. He must have taken the revolver . . . What did they say, Mélanie?"

"They're coming in a car."

"Keep quiet, Jean! They'll be here in a minute. It's not worthwhile risking—"

It was precisely because it was not worthwhile that he did it. To stay quietly waiting was to make himself look ridiculous; whereas if he marched across the yard with his hands in his pockets and boldly entered the garage, he would arouse admiration.

He had not yet disappeared when there was the sound of a second shot. Mme Fernand, in her turn, ran across to the door, and called to him, staring into the half-darkness:

"Jean!"

"What?"

He was standing in the middle of the garage, facing the ladder.

"Come out of there! Don't expose yourself for no reason."

They heard the noise of a police car, and soon the sergeant entered the yard, with Mélanie showing him the way. At that moment a third shot was fired, and Monsieur Jean, forcing himself to move as slowly as possible, left the garage.

"I think he's firing into the air," he remarked. "If it's my revolver, it only has six bullets. So he has only three left."

"What makes you think he's gone mad?" the sergeant asked Mme Fernand.

"I don't know. He's always been strange. Just now I went to ask him something, and he shouted to me not to come near."

The sun was high and cars were passing. The neighbors probably mistook the detonations for the backfiring of engines. However, the butcher from across the road, in his red-stained apron, entered the yard, intrigued by the presence of the police.

The little group, including Mélanie, whose hands were still greasy with dishwater, was gathered a few yards from the open doorway of the garage. The hens and the cock, frightened by the noise, squawked in angry manifestation of their disapproval.

The sergeant, who looked enormous, approached the entrance, leaned against the doorpost and, thrusting his head a little way forward, called:

"Hey, old Félix! You're going to behave yourself, aren't you? I warn you that if you fire again I shall fire back!"

Félix fired, but only hit a kettle hanging on the wall.

"So that's it! You want to make trouble, do you? Well, we shall see."

When the sergeant turned his head, it could be seen that he was joking.

"We've only got to let him get rid of the last two bullets," he said in a low voice and with a wink.

The butcher asked:

"Who is it?"

"Félix," replied Mélanie.

It was strange to be there, looking into the wide-open door of the garage, where, even if one thrust one's head inside, one could see nothing.

They waited without knowing exactly what they were waiting for. The postman, who had just arrived, with his box on his stomach, stayed with the others, and Nine was standing behind the window in the kitchen.

But she was not thinking about Félix. She was talking to Rose, who had come in and sat down. She asked her:

"What are you going to do?"

The girl answered, mistrustfully:

"About what?"

"About what Mme Fernand told you."

"So you know about it, too? Well, if everybody knows, there's no point in making a mystery of it. What am I going to do? The moment they give me money for the doctor . . ."

Out in the yard it was almost like a game, with just a sufficient element of danger to make it exciting. The policeman who had accompanied the sergeant, jealous of his superior, had also crossed over to the doorway. There he gave the onlookers a significant nod. Then he got out his revolver and aimed at the kettle that had already been hit.

He fired. The man above, invisible because he was stretched out on his mattress, replied.

Mme Fernand glanced covertly at her husband, and knew that this did not please him. It was true that they were rather like a party at a fair, or on a street watching someone climb a tree to rescue a budgerigar that had escaped from its mistress.

Monsieur Jean, noting that Félix had only one bullet left, moved forward. Perhaps he would not have minded being wounded? The sergeant tried to stop him in the doorway.

"Be careful, Monsieur Jean."

The proprietor released himself and vanished. No one could have explained his reasons for this display of resolution. And the sergeant would have found it difficult to define the authority under which he was acting.

Monsieur Jean, floundering through the straw and muck, slowly reached the foot of the ladder, with a fierce determination not to let himself be stopped.

There was a cry from outside at the sound of another shot. Mme Fernand rushed forward crying:

"Jean! Jean!"

He turned around.

"What is it?"

"You aren't wounded?"

"Not on your life!"

He released himself for a second time and climbed the ladder, at last setting foot on the gallery where Félix had established his den.

He could be seen from below, at first standing upright, then bending down, then upright again, with his head lowered, staring at his hand. No one dared say anything. They waited. And he himself did not know what words to use.

"Perhaps he ought to be moved," he finally growled.

It was difficult, because Félix was heavy and the ladder unsteady. Fortunately, the sergeant was strong and wasn't worried about getting his uniform dirty.

"Where shall we put him?"

"In one of the bedrooms."

"Rose! Isn't number 3 vacant?"

"Yes, madame, but I haven't done the room yet."

Mme Fernand asked her husband in a low voice, "Is he dead?"

Monsieur Jean chose not to answer. He did not know, not having ventured to touch the body again. He held his bloodstained hand well away from him. When he reached the house, he held his hand under the faucet and watched with wide eyes the stream of pink liquid that flowed from it.

"Hello . . . Dr. Chevrel? . . . This is the White Horse. . . . Yes, a matter of the utmost urgency."

The sergeant stayed up above, while the policeman came down and announced:

"It seems that his heart's beating."

"It's not possible," groaned Mme Fernand, who was trying not to faint. "It is not possible that Félix can still be alive, with half his head blown off!"

They had reached the stage when no one dared look at anyone else. Fists were clenched. People started to move and then stopped for no reason.

Why had the doctor not arrived?

The sergeant, white-faced, descended a few rungs of the ladder and stopped halfway down.

"You've sent for the doctor? ... Tell me, was he a Catholic?"

Glances were exchanged, but no one knew.

"No harm in sending for the priest," Mélanie remarked.

"Do you know him?"

"He prepared my daughter for her first communion. I'll go."

Chevrel drove into the yard as usual in his little car.

"Who is it?" he asked.

"Félix. He's up there. He's shot himself in the head."

"In that case I'll need my surgical case. Someone will have to call my house."

"Rose will do it. You understand, Rose? You must ask for the doctor's surgical case."

Mme Fernand had regained her self-control. It was necessary. Every now and then she looked at her husband, pleased, on the whole, to see him so shattered. Although it was impossible to say it, or even to think it directly, the drama had done him good. His crisis was now over. He had dropped into a chair and was staring straight in front of him, still with a dazed look, but one in which there was no longer any panic.

The sergeant, who had now come down, lit a pipe with a curved stem and remarked:

"I was right. He's not dead. . . . I suppose I couldn't have a fairly stiff drink?"

His hands were also bloodstained, but this did not worry him. He downed two glasses of alcohol, smacking his lips, before installing himself at a table and getting out his notebook. Although not proposing to go to work immediately, he did not mind assuming an official attitude.

"Incidentally, why did he do it?" he suddenly asked.

It surprised him that he had not thought of this before. It had seemed quite natural to lay siege to the garage, but no one had asked why they should be after old Félix.

"He must have had an attack," said Mme Fernand, after glancing at her husband.

"A attack of what?"

"Of madness. He was a sick man. The doctor had been to see him."

A door opened on the floor above, and Chevrel called:

"Will someone telephone for an ambulance?"

"Telephone where?" asked Mme Fernand, not knowing.

Everyone was bathed in sunshine. It was the hour when the sun penetrated at an oblique angle into the café and the dining room.

"Nevers 127 . . . No! La Charité 12. That'll be quicker."

Rose returned, with a small flat bag.

"Take it upstairs."

"I'm afraid to."

Mélanie took it, and did not come down again, Chevrel having enlisted her services.

While his wife was telephoning, Monsieur Jean got up and went to the counter in the café, thinking to pour himself a drink, but on the point of picking up a bottle, he shrugged his shoulders. What was the use?

Eyes were watching him from a distance. His wife was keeping him under observation, and he was no longer in the mood to rebel.

"If he's sent for an ambulance, that means there's still a chance," the sergeant pronounced. "Although, after seeing him, I could have sworn . . ."

The policeman, seated astride a chair, was rolling a cigarette.

A calm that was almost unreal now prevailed in the White Horse. It might have been the winter season, when they were lucky to serve three meals a day, and the time was spent huddled around the stove waiting for customers. Monsieur Jean surprised himself by catching a fly. Then, for no definite reason, like someone on the defensive, he strayed toward his wife, approaching her step by step.

He was watching her. A single look, or the vaguest of smiles, would have been enough to bring him to a stop, but Mme Fernand knew him and waited for him without appearing to wait.

"Forgive me," he murmured as he passed.

That was all. The rest would be for the night, when he would begin to cry. For he would certainly cry, not for her sake or on account of Félix, but for himself. He would begin by saying:

"Do you think this is a life for a man my age?"

He wanted everything, the cars that drove past and the countries that awaited him, the women who dined under his roof and those whose photographs he saw in the papers. His desires sometimes became so overwhelming that he was capable of dancing with rage, like a child.

He had murmured:

"Forgive me."

That would last a few weeks, perhaps even months. It

was no use expecting more. Mme Fernand was satisfied to the extent that she quite forgot why they were all there waiting in silence while the sergeant's clogged pipe made an unpleasant bubbling noise every time he drew on it.

It was like something that had happened almost every day when Mme Fernand's father had had a few drinks and tugged at his mustache while he looked about him with angry eyes. Yet that had lasted forty years, because his wife, although she was quite small, had remained calm, never weeping or showing that she was afraid. At the height of a quarrel—because these broke out sometimes among the customers—she was not afraid to say:

"Go on, Hector! Go to bed." And it was she who had the last word.

She said to her daughter, in her peasant accent:

"I'd sooner have that than someone with tuberculosis, like Aunt Berthe's husband."

Aunt Berthe had spent her life looking after not only her husband but also her three children, who were all infected.

"Provided one keeps one's health!"

A big white ambulance adorned with a red cross pulled up in front of the terrace, and people emerged. Mélanie came downstairs.

"The doctor wants the stretcher to be taken up."

In half an hour at the most, customers would start arriving. Nine, who knew this, had relighted the fire and, as a precaution, had put a stew and a pot of beans on the stove. She was not crying, but she sniffed as she looked at the yard, where now there was only the dog, stretched unhappily at the full length of its chain, incapable of understanding.

Two men went up with the stretcher, and came down with some difficulty, for the stairway was narrow. Everybody had a look as they passed, but the head of the wounded man was smothered in bandages. The doctor, looking very tired, paused to rest in the café. The priest, who had just arrived, was talking outside to the men from the ambulance.

"He didn't say anything?" asked Monsieur Jean, facing the wall.

Chevrel shrugged his shoulders in a way that made one shiver. Having drunk a single glass of marc, he said:

"Half his tongue was shot off."

"Be quiet!" cried Rose, and fled into the kitchen.

They were hoisting Félix into the ambulance.

"He put the muzzle of the gun in his mouth."

The engine was running. The ambulance drove off.

"Do you think he was mad?"

"Why?"

Yes, why should Félix have been mad?

"I was thinking . . ." the sergeant began. But what was the use of trying to explain? Chevrel had a headache, and he still had to telephone to La Charité.

"I'll send you my report," he said impatiently to the sergeant.

A car drew up, and a plump lady and gentleman got out of it. Mme Fernand exclaimed:

"Jean!"

He understood at once and shut the door of the café so that the customers would not see the police. Mme Fernand went to her desk and just had time to adopt a suitable countenance.

"Can we have dinner right away?"

"Certainly! You can have whatever you like. I'll tell my husband. Rose, tell Monsieur . . ."

He came, automatically running over in his mind what

was left in the refrigerator. A moment later he was bent over his stove, and Nine was saying:

"I put the stew on the fire. Also the beans, for the leg of mutton."

A prod with the poker. Then he picked up his white cap from the table and put it on his head.

"Will it take long?" asked the customers.

"Not at all! You'll be served in no time. Mélanie! Set two places for this lady and gentleman."

Life was resuming its normal course, and yet one was already conscious of an emptiness. Impossible not to think of the garage, where now there was no one, and there was the big white ambulance speeding along the highway.

"Rose! Go and ask your father if he would like to come here for a day or two to act as night porter while we're looking around for someone. You know where to find him?"

"Yes, I know. I'll bring him if he's not too drunk."

The striped awning was let down a little farther, because the sun, now sinking low, was uncomfortable for the two customers.

11

Emile had thin legs, big knees, and an overlong neck. As they walked along the path, he slashed with a stick at the nettles and explained to Christian, who had become a nice little boy of eight:

"You understand, don't you? If they let me join the Boy Scouts I won't have to do any jobs on Sundays."

"And what about me?" asked Christian innocently.

"When you're a bit bigger, I'll take you on as a wolf cub."

"How long will that be?"

Emile reflected with manly gravity and replied:

"Next year."

"Watch your feet, Emile," his father said to him, for he had a habit of walking with his toes turned out, which wore his heels on one side.

The sun was sinking. The dust made one thirsty. The Loire was alive with little sparkles of light, which dazzled the eyes.

"Perhaps we chose a rather long walk," said Mama, who had difficulty keeping up.

Father apologized. "I expected it to be much shorter. I forgot about this big bend in the river. Would you like to stop and rest?"

"It's not worth it now. We're practically there."

Mama had grown thick around the waist, and Emile had not been particularly gratified to learn that soon he would have a new little brother or sister.

"I hope it's a girl," he had said, although no one knew why.

Christian said nothing; he never said anything. He went through the world with the same dreamy expression that he had had when, at the age of four, he had been carried on his father's shoulders. He had now been at school for two years and had had nothing but bad reports. "Lack of attention," wrote his teacher in red ink. Was he looking at the blackboard or at the two pigeons perched on the roof of the school?

Because the sun was burning the back of his neck, Father had spread a handkerchief, which hung from under his hat.

"You're sure you wouldn't like to rest for a minute?"

"No, really."

"You must remember that the doctor said walking is good for you."

She smiled faintly, an indulgent smile, and refrained from remarking that there are walks and walks, and that a dozen kilometers was a pretty long way for a pregnant woman.

"We could have something to eat before we take the bus."

"What would be the sense of that? It costs money, and we shall be home very quickly."

"Just as you please."

Two or three times, without seeming to do so, she glanced at him, and she sensed his excitement at the idea that they were coming to Pouilly and that they would pass the White Horse Inn. The evidence of this was that as they went along the lane leading to the highway, they were walking more quickly, without his realizing it.

"Your feet, Emile!"

"Yes, Mama." And Emile explained to his brother:

"When I'm a Scout, I'll play soccer. But I'll have special shoes."

Christian was sleepy. Sleepy and hungry, because with him the two needs were closely linked.

"Aren't you thirsty?" asked Arbelet, in a voice that caused his wife to smile.

"Are you?"

"Well, I admit . . ."

He was taking precautions. He could not pass in front of the White Horse and simply ignore it, and he was clumsily paving the way.

"It's not so much the heat as the dust. Anyway, the sausage was too salty. It wasn't like it usually is."

"We'll stop and have a drink."

Another hundred yards. The road ran in front of them, blue with oil and gasoline. Cars passed.

"Careful, children! Stay close to us! Emile, take your brother's hand."

They crossed over. The laurels were still there, no doubt the same ones, in the same barrels cut in half and painted green. There was also the same straight-backed bench, green like the rest, and the orange-and-white awning.

"Shall we sit here?"

She replied, "Why not?"

"You're not afraid that your uncle . . . ?"

A flush appeared on Arbelet's cheeks when he heard the footsteps of a waitress crossing the café, and he hesitated to look around when she emerged. But it was not Rose. It was a new girl, whom he did not know.

"What will you have?"

"I'd like some beer," said Germaine.

"Two small beers and an orangeade for the children."

"One for each of us!" demanded Emile, who was generally obliged to share everything with his brother.

"Very well. Two orangeades," Father conceded.

The sun was red and the shadows blue, particularly under the green of the table. Arbelet was searching for a pretext to enter the house and yard, but he disliked the idea of resorting to the obvious reason. Still, he wanted to see . . .

Not necessarily Rose, or the other girl, the older one, whose name was Thérèse. Nor was he looking for his wife's uncle, or any detail in particular, but simply for the atmosphere, of which he had retained a more vivid memory than of places where he had lived for years.

He heard the sound of tables being set, and the voices of people playing cards, but kept his head averted for fear of giving himself away. Nevertheless, Germaine understood, and she said to him in a low voice, because of the children:

"You might go and ask if Félix is still here."

"You think so?"

He got up awkwardly and passed through the café into the dining room, where Mme Fernand was seated at her desk, so exactly as she had been four years earlier that it was amazing.

"Can I do something for you?"

The kitchen door was open. As to what he wanted, he could not have said. He simply wanted to go in and look at everything and smell everything, to recapture for a moment that life which had once seemed to him ideal. Why? For no reason. That was how it was.

"Is your husband well?"

She looked closely at him and murmured:

"Excuse me. I don't seem to remember you."

"The man who was hit with a bottle."

He lowered his head, since he thought a faint scar, half hidden by his hair, could be plainly seen.

"I'll go and call my husband."

Because she really didn't remember. Perhaps there had been other occasions when people had been hit on the head with a siphon.

"Jean! Come here a moment."

He came, wiping his face with his towel, and looked attentively at the customer.

"Wait. I think . . ."

"Arbelet, from Nevers . . . It was the time when a Pole, who was the husband of one of your waitresses . . ."

"Ah, yes . . ." But this was said out of politeness, and he hurried on, as though to dismiss the subject, "What can I get you?"

"Nothing, thank you. I'm being served on the terrace. I'm with my family. . . . Incidentally, do you still have a certain Félix, who—"

"He's probably in the yard."

"Would you allow me—"

"Of course! This way. That's right. I see you remember the way."

As if he remembered! The blood had mounted to his head, and he felt ill at ease, as though he had committed a crime. When he was gone, Mme Fernand asked:

"Who is he?"

"A fellow who got knocked on the head with a siphon. His wife came to fetch him the next day."

Monsieur Jean was going through a bad period, because he had developed a passion for fly fishing and business prevented him from going to the river every morning. He regarded the customers as his enemies and himself as their victim, as though he were a slave. He had again lost weight, and his eyes had grown gloomy and dark-ringed. It happened in stages. At other times he put on weight and played cards with the customers or shopkeepers and listened to the radio. Now he was again beginning to look disdainfully at people and to grow angry at trifles.

A woman entered, seeming to apologize for her advanced state of pregnancy.

"Excuse me, madame. Is my husband here?" She had told the children not to move from the bench.

"I think he's in the yard. He wanted news of Félix."

"He's still with you?"

"Oh, yes."

They were looking each other over, neither needing any words to understand the other.

"I must tell you something. Félix Drouin is a relation, an uncle who has gone downhill."

"Ah!"

"I wanted to do something for him. Four years ago I sent my husband to offer him . . ."

They noted the back of a waitress, clad in black, with a white apron, who was arranging fruit in small baskets.

"I understand."

"My uncle would not accept."

"I know."

"You know?"

"Well, anyway, I know that he wouldn't leave this place at any price."

They were both well brought up. They had their reticences. Neither wished to upset the other, or to touch on matters about which it was better not to speak.

The air was clear and resonant as crystal. They could hear the voice of Emile solemnly explaining to Christian the workings of the new types of car. A dog barked somewhere in the yard. A poker rattled amid the coal of the cooking stove.

"You don't have too much trouble with him?"

"With Monsieur Félix?" She referred to him as "Monsieur" because the lady had confessed that he was her uncle. "We scarcely ever see him. He insists upon living in his own corner like a savage. He's an eccentric."

"Yes . . . Well, thank you very much."

"Do you want to see him?"

"No, I'd just as soon not. It might not please him."

Mme Fernand now clearly remembered the woman who one morning had come in search of her husband and had borne him off in a matter of minutes. She had no inclination to laugh or even to smile. At the most she envied her her state of pregnancy, because she herself had tried in vain to have a child, who would perhaps have settled everything. But who could say that this lady had not wanted the child because . . .

"At that time you had a little maidservant, very young . . ."

"You mean Rose? She's married now. Her husband has a garage eight kilometers from here, in the direction of Nevers."

She had not been mistaken. The lady was jealous! And the husband, under the pretext of seeing Félix, was trying to find Rose, or her ghost.

Germaine blushed for no reason, as though she sensed instinctively that she had given herself away.

"There's a bus for Nevers in a few minutes, isn't there?"

"In a quarter of an hour."

Monsieur Jean had come to look at her through the half-open door, but he had not recognized her.

"Thank you, madame. Good evening."

"Good evening, madame."

There was nothing for it but to go back to the bench on the terrace, where Emile was still talking about cars to his brother, who was half asleep.

"Is Father coming?"

"He'll be here in a minute, dear."

She did not consider herself more intelligent or stronger than the average woman. She was always a little afraid, but it was no use showing it.

She recognized her husband's footsteps. She did not look around when he sat down beside her, but simply asked:

"Did you see him?"

"Yes."

They had to talk in low voices because of the children.

"I don't know what's happened to him. I could hardly recognize him. His face was all out of shape, and he could barely speak. It looked as though he had had an injury."

"What did he say to you?"

"Nothing . . . I'll tell you later."

"But he doesn't want to?"

"Want to what?"

"Want us to help him get into a home . . . get him out of this place."

Why was there a hint of agitation in Arbelet's voice as he replied?

"No indeed."

As though they were talking about himself! Or as though he understood!

"It's time for the bus."

"Mademoiselle! How much do I owe you?"

She was a rather lifeless blonde, with dull eyes.

"I'll go and ask."

So she was new.

"Eight francs seventy-five."

They strolled past the houses, Emile walking with one foot in the gutter and the other on the curb. The sun was playing a symphony of light and color, and sometimes, even on the highway, there was a puff of air redolent of all the countryside.

"Emile, your feet."

Christian looked up and complained:

"I'm hungry."

The bakery was opposite. They bought two small chocolate cakes and then stood waiting for the bus, which was late.

"What did he say?"

"Uncle Félix?"

In fact, he had said what he usually said, "Hell, shit, and damnation!" But one could no longer distinguish the words because of the injury to his jaw. He was dirty. His beard no longer grew on certain patches of skin. His feet could no longer be got into shoes or slippers and seemed to be wrapped in rags.

"Just the same, I'll have to . . ."

Mme Fernand assured customers alarmed by his looks that he was quite harmless. And when Monsieur Jean entered the cellar, he turned his head and muttered to the old man:

"If you open the door or try to see anything . . ."

That was the last straw. Félix grunted like a beaten dog and went and curled up on his mattress, sniffing.

"When I'm grown up," said Emile in the bus . . . He knew that his parents, on the seat behind them, were discussing a serious matter. Father concluded:

"Well, he wants it that way, doesn't he?"

Mama did not reply, but sat gazing out at the countryside without disclosing her thoughts.

She might have talked to the proprietress at the White Horse. They would have understood one another. But even if she had had the chance, she probably would not have taken it.

One does not talk about these things. . . .

One adapts oneself. . . .

One does the best one can. . . .

Thus Arbelet, free to pursue his own thoughts, was beginning to look dreamy.

"When will you go to see the manager about the raise?" she hastened to ask.

He had to make an effort.

"On Wednesday. We're all agreed. We're going to . . ."

Down there at Pouilly, left behind them on the road . . .

"We'll have supper as soon as we get home, my dears. It just needs warming up."

Her stomach felt heavy, but that did not matter.

Mme Fernand, opening the kitchen door, saw at once that her husband was not there, nor was the new maid.

"Has Yvonne gone for the wine?" she asked.

The answer was yes. Nine gazed vaguely into the yard.

It is enough to understand one another. Moreover, it is useless to let the fact be known.